HOOLIGANS

By
Matthew R Walker

Lava Publishing
Bend, Oregon

Also by Matthew R Walker

Migration

Soon to be released

Patrol Boat
Pacific Peril
U-31
Western Pacific

This is a work of fiction. All of the characters, organizations, and events portrayed in this novel are either products of the author's imagination or used fictitiously with a great deal of research to stay true and as close to the actual events as possible.

Published by: Lava Publishing, LLC.
Print Edition

For information, address: Lava Publishing, 500 W Harbor Dr #804 San Diego, CA 92101.

http://www.lavapublishing.com
Walker, Matthew R
Hooligans / Matthew R Walker –1st U.S. ed.
ISBN-978-1-62003-004-2 print
ISBN-978-1-62003-002-8 and
978-1-62003-003-5 electronic format

This book is dedicated to Max

and

The men who sailed as volunteers in the

United States Coast Guard Corsair Fleet

© Walt Disney 1942

Acknowledgements

An author can never take full credit for his or her work because there are so many people that contribute to the success of a written body of work. In this case I would like to thank Barbara who offered much encouragement and critique; my life-long friend, Dave, for his support and taking time to read my manuscripts in the roughest form; for the double check on the nautical authenticity I need to thank Hugh; and finally, Rachelle, my publisher who dedicated many hours to ensure its success.

One

It did not ascend.

It did not descend.

Its eye protruded from the black Atlantic.

The monster rested motionless.

The ocean did not notice the creature's existence waves passed over-head, fish swam around it ignorant of the danger.

Its black skin cold, like the sea it occupied.

It emitted no noise, unless you were to hold a stethoscope to its rigid chest, faint internal functions might be audible.

The creature held its breath, waiting.

Its only function was to kill. Not for survival, but out of hunger, not for itself, but to feed a larger and greater thing that was growing.

The ocean current was, at present, its only mode of propulsion. It drifted ten feet below the choppy surface at four knots. An appendage grew out of the body and stood erect. The limb held the creature's eye. It used the eye to find its prey that floated on the surface. Like a lion crouched in the tall grass of the Serengeti, waiting for a gazelle to pass close enough to pounce, the monster of the underwater waited.

Once it found its prey it came alive, lowered its eye down into its bosom and sped headfirst like a bullet into attack.

Its optical umbilical on the surface scanned, searched for the catch.

Two

Night was fading, a gentle swell swept in from a storm far away to the east and the horizon started to show faint evidence of the approaching day. The painted pink underside of cumulus clouds appeared in the distance. The *R. P. Resor* sailed up the New Jersey coast, just another freighter cruising toward New York, but to Captain Fred Marcus she was everything, his alternate life and the mistress of his heart. He had made the passage up the eastern United States coast countless times over the years. *R. P. Resor* carried almost everything imaginable, oil, cotton, wheat, machinery, and once a load of South American tarantulas for the Bronx Zoo. More than any other time, the excitement and suspense reached out and grabbed you like a protagonist's walk to the attic in a suspense movie. The United States was at war, and German U-boats sank sixty-nine freighters since the war began two months earlier. Captain Marcus would not lose his ship to the Nazis bastards.

Leaning his heavy arms on the rail, Captain Marcus peered out with his piercing black eyes. The black wool coat hung open at the front and his white sweater, stained from six years of wear, fit odd accidently tucked into his corduroy trousers. White streaks in his dark hair and beard suggested his age. He had been an officer in the Navy during the Great War, serving his time aboard a four-stack destroyer patrolling the west Coast of Ireland. After the war Captain Marcus got his Merchant Marine license and started work for Macaw Transport Ltd. in New Orleans. He tried operating his own shipping company, transporting southern lumber north, but after only two years he went broke. Now, with more than thirty-four years at sea, Captain Marcus was ready to retire. However the war kept him at it. Retirement could wait.

Before sailing, Captain Marcus mustered his officers in his cabin to go over the Navy procedures for submarine avoidance. He was relieved that a Navy detail was on board to man the newly installed 3-inch deck gun.

He had an indefatigable faith that *R. P. Resor* would survive the war.

Captain Marcus looked at the logbook for the new watch, 0400-0800 27 February 1942. His second officer was on watch. Captain Marcus couldn't sleep, which was not unusual for the seafarer, but the early morning gave him an especially uneasy feeling. With the moon now below the horizon, the stars clung to life as the approaching dawn threaten their existence. It was a clear night, save for the cumulus clouds on the horizon. Captain Marcus brought his gaze back down from the heavens to notice the faint lights from the New Jersey coast off the port side as the *R. P. Resor* steamed north.

From the port bridgewing Captain Marcus looked back at his dark ship. She was ghostly. The wake zigzagged behind her, a phosphorescent tail fading into nothingness.

"Your coffee, sir."

"Thank you, Seaman Alder."

Seaman Alder wandered back toward the other seaman ready to turn the watch.

Captain Marcus overheard them battling about which sailor had had the most boastful, erotic encounter ashore. Able Seaman Signaut seemed to have won with a tale about a whore he visited in the French Quarter; the Captain attempted to picture the scene as Signaut described it.

"All's you kids wanna do is screw," Second Officer Gerhard said, quieting the young seamen. Gerhard was thirty years past his prime. Thirty years past the thought of having a whore whirling around in a basket dropped down on him.

Alder replied, "So?"

Captain Marcus turned away, sipped his coffee with one hand and pulled his coat together with the other. He was a man that could not believe that he too was once that occupied with sex. He thought of Roxanne. Had he been that overcome with sexual desire when he met his wife? He smiled and thought of the naked woman who had walked him to the backdoor, how she had leaned down to pet the cat on the head, she looked more delicious than he could ever remember. Roxanne pulled him back into the house and they had enjoyed a moment that

Marcus savored in his thoughts. Afterwards, she stood at the screen door and waved good-bye to her sea captain— never had he felt so attracted to a woman. He still felt that way, the moving, uplifting appetite of those young seamen was something he had not outgrown, and hoped he never would. Being at sea gave his marriage wonderful, passionate homecomings. He wasn't home long enough to get neither bored, nor irritated with Roxanne's constant presence and particulars. He had the fondest and most untainted thoughts of his wife. With all the flare and sensitivity of a dime novel simile, the beauty of the night reminded him of the beauty of his Roxanne.

He smiled.

Roxanne would love the gentle rolling, soothing swells and crisp effortless breeze and stars that illuminated the night just enough as not to expose any of its imperfections.

"Captain, changing course right ten degrees rudder."

Captain nodded to the elder Mr. Gerhard, who maintained the prescribed zigzag pattern.

"Seaman Alder, would you be so kind as to take those Navy boys some coffee. It must be cold up on the foc's'l," Captain Marcus asked.

"Aye, aye, sir. It's cold all right. My watch up there was colder than a well-digger's ass." Alder poured the coffee into a Thermos, "Those lights are like Christmas all over again. New Jersey has more lights than I bet the whole state of Louisiana."

"Yes, it is bright," Captain Marcus replied, confident staying close to shore, dark, and zigzagging that no German U-boat would dare attack. The New Jersey lights were a comfort to everyone on the ship, like a child afraid of the dark, the coast was a hallway night-light that brought protection through the crack of a partially open bedroom door. To the east lurked a dark vastness filled with unknown monsters, but one quick look back to the west brought reassurance and safety found in that comforting glow from the New Jersey shoreline. Every seaman aboard felt it, the ship felt it.

He could feel life in his ship. She had a soul. That is what every seaman thought of his ship, and it was no different with an intelligent, educated man like Captain Marcus. The girl weighed twenty thousand tons with 78,729 barrels of fuel oil and fifty men on board. She carried them as a mother carried her son.

Abruptly, the bridge phone rang. It was Forsdal, reporting a small vessel off the starboard bow.

"You've a good eye. Thanks, mate." Captain Marcus was proud of his merchant crew. They were good, alert and capable men. He trusted them, as did they trust their captain. Captain Marcus looked through the glass but couldn't spot the vessel. He walked out to the starboard side bridge wing to get a better view and was instantly struck by the wintry air that iced his nostrils.

The creature was motionless. Its eye could see the costal lights forming the horizon. A small blank space on the coast was the only break in the line of brightness. The void swallowed another lamp and spat out a light behind it—a shadow moving down the coast.

Prey.

The creature came alive.

Three

A green 1939 Lincoln sped south on Route 36.

Luther Rogers looked down at the speedometer, forty-five, better slow down. The headlights illuminated the sign for Sandy Hook. It was rare that Luther drove, he usually sat in the back with a newspaper as Jimmy chauffeured him about, but Jimmy didn't come in until six and when he heard about the torpedoed freighter early this morning he decided to drive himself.

The east sky glowed red, the illumination very different from the amber cloud that hung over New York City. Luther Rogers knew the city, could not imagine living anywhere else. It was winter so he lived in the Fifth Avenue brownstone, and it had taken him two hours to get here. His view of the night sky from his frequent sojourns outside the city had always included the skyline, the soft glow of light, the galactic draw from that beacon of life that shown upwards, outward. The Broadway marquees, the flashing signs of Times Square, the streetlamps, brothel lights, the city was alive and Luther Rogers did not want to imagine what the sky or life would be like without the halo of the City.

He glanced out to sea at the unnatural red-yellow light that burst with an occasional flash from an explosion. He parked the Lincoln in the row of onlookers next to the last car, a 1923 model A. The people that crowded the beach that morning stared off into the east where flames and a trail of dark smoke contrasted against the rising sun hidden behind soft grey clouds. Luther noticed one family had brought chairs and a basket of food. The woman in a blue flowered dress, tailored to hide her obesity, spread out a blanket and tried to feed three children scampering around uninterested in the spectacle just a few miles offshore. Her husband sat in a wicker foldaway with his hat pushed back on his head, one hand balanced a child's telescope and the other hand holding half of a ham and cheese sandwich.

Luther Rogers reached into the big Lincoln and produced binoculars from the glove box. He brought the binoculars up to his eyes and took a few minutes to adjust the focus, it had been years since he last used this old pair that Jimmy had thrown into the Lincoln when it had arrived from the showroom. He saw a dark form spitting out flames and smoke—*R. P. Resor* was burning, illuminating a grave. Luther learned later that only two crewmen survived out of the fifty merchant and Navy sailors aboard.

"Hey, mister. . . can I take a look?"

Luther, his mind filled with a tidal wave of emotion and concentration, handed his binoculars to the teenager.

He carved a picture of the doomed freighter in his thoughts. Slowly, the significance of the incident poured over him. His attention preoccupied about the ill-fated crew, Luther wondered if anyone could possibly survive as the onlookers continued the annoying distraction of sophomoric gesticulations. All these people gawking, nobody bothering to help as the ship burned, about three miles from shore Luther guessed, so close, yet unreachable. He became disgusted with himself for participating in the perverse spectacle. A wave of distress, passion, patriotism, whatever the hell you wanted to call it, ripped through him like a grappling hook being dragged through his insides by a truck.

Then it hit him—the Germans are in United States waters, the German navy is in the United States! The war was something told in newspapers about far away and exotic places, China, Czechoslovakia, Warsaw, Manchuria, Burma, and New Guinea. He felt a personal invasion as if the Nazis where in his living room. The fear and horror of the war so close scared Luther, there was no other way to describe it. He was sure he could hear the screams, the merchant sailors shrieking from the pain and suffering. What a horrible death. A cold shiver of panic and fear overcame him. Was this war?

"Eeee, I'll get you." Three children ran past him squealing. It was sacrilegious. This was a funeral not a carnival.

"Sir, sir! Your binoculars! Hey mister!" The boy called after the stranger.

Luther Rogers didn't hear the cries to return his glasses, he didn't remember starting the engine. The binoculars landed on the passenger seat through the open window as he backed out in a cloud of dust the boy smiled and waved.

The Lincoln swerved left and then stabilized as the big car's tires met the asphalt road. Luther was on the board of directors for American Telephone and Telegraph, one of the few companies to prosper in the last decade. He was a man used to making decisions based on facts, money, and rock solid judgment. Now, irrational, careless, passion-filled staccato thoughts hit him like machine gun fire. He knew what he had to do.

He gunned the big green Lincoln up the highway with recklessness. The V8 roared as Luther shifted through the gears. The speedometer inched up to seventy-five. Luther turned off toward the Holland tunnel and rolled through the tool booth without coming to a complete stop. It was the start of the morning traffic for Manhattan and Luther got in line with the rest of the vehicles going into the city. Once through the tunnel he fought his way to the brownstone on Fifth. Luckily, there was a parking space in front. He veered into the gap and then jammed on the brakes, parking a little cockeyed, but good enough. Two steps at a time, he stormed up the steps and slammed the door shut behind him. The light was dim and Luther did not wait for his eyes to adjust, instead he strode into the study, reached behind the small bar, and poured gin into a highball glass. He slammed down a mouthful and then plopped down into an overstuffed chair. Swallowed in the soft upholstery of the chair, the glass of gin gripped in his trembling hand, Luther finally sighed. He consciously took in a few deep breaths to calm himself—it worked. Luther stared into the glass of gin and then softly placed it on a lace doily under a lamp on the end table. Forcing himself to sit back, he stretched his legs out and with a compulsory calmness—the placidity that he was known for in the

business world—and contemplated his
next move.

Four

The clanking of typewriters, whirling electric fans, rustle of papers, even the scratch of pencils across the paper added to the cacophony of the office. The ambient noise of a busy office was nothing foreign to Luther. He adjusted himself for the umpteenth time as he leafed through the two month-old Newsweek, not really reading but occupying the moment with distraction, doing something instead of watching the second hand on the clock mounted above the receptionist. She wore a red high collar dress with white lace sleeves, on anyone else it would have taken a man's breath away, but the receptionist had an expression that refused to allow her thin lips a smile. Her whole body stiff as if she had an ironing board stuck up her ass, Luther thought. The clock ticked. It had been a tumultuous week of rumination since the scene on the beach. Luther threw the Newsweek back onto the low coffee table; it skidded across a Life magazine before coming to a stop. He picked up his grey homburg, gripped the edge and moved it hand-to-hand in circles, deciding whether or not to leave. Young officers, wearing naval uniforms, hurried past. Each had the look of determination, a war-winning-solutions-buried-deep-within gaze plastered on their faces. Luther shifted once again in the wood chair that had become painfully uncomfortable. He was not a man accustomed to waiting. He made other people wait.

"Excuse me, miss? How much longer? Does the Admiral know I'm here?" Luther Rogers showed his irritation and immediately regretted the discourteous display.

The receptionist cracked something she thought would pass as a smile; her brown teeth offered no relief.

Luther wanted to stand and march through the cheap frame door into Admiral Andrews' office and scream like a young school child for attention, was this how it felt to wait?

Just as he was about to show the Navy who Luther Rogers, director of American Telephone and Telegraph, was a man of about forty caught his eye and walked toward him. The man wore a dark blazer with four gold strips on his sleeve ends, he held out his hand. Luther took it and pumped with relief.

"Mister Rogers? I'm Captain Kurtz, Admiral Andrews' Chief of Staff. A pleasure to meet you, sir. I apologize for the wait."

"Oh, no bother, really." Luther said.

"If you'll follow me we'll go see the Admiral now."

Luther Rogers nodded his approval and followed the Captain, but not through the door he had suspected to be the Admiral's office. Instead they headed down a long corridor. Walking past doorways where Luther could see men and women working furiously with paper. Paper in typewriters, on desks, posted on corkboards, on tabletops, on maps, and in the air, it was everywhere. Each room they passed appeared to be in some sort of chaos, each unique to the other. Luther Rogers recognized some of his own AT&T equipment—the new Teletype machines spat out yet more paper.

Captain Kurtz stopped at a plain pine door and gripped the knob, smiling at Luther as he did so, and then with the theatrical flair of Douglas Fairbanks, he threw open the door.

The effect was lost.

Inside, a man of about sixty was surrounded by more young men in uniforms that appeared to be clones of the men in the rest of the building. The Admiral did not take notice of Kurtz or his guest. The office was surprisingly small, Luther Rogers' secretary had an office twice this size. A small window, with curtains drawn, offered a crack of sunlight that sent a stream of yellow across the back of the leather chair and oak colonial desk. Nautical brass lamps hung from the ceiling in the four corners. On each side of the window the walls were decorated with the Admiral's face—pictures of the admiral posing with men and ships Luther couldn't identify. Two doors broke the wall on the left, one door on the right.

Men in uniforms, like painted figures of a coo-coo clock, appeared, dropped more paper on the desk, and then existed. What was beyond the doors? Luther could only imagine some giant machine spitting out paper, he wondered where it all came from. The businessman in him made a quick calculation of the cost and logistics of supplying this naval office.

"Excuse me, Admiral? I have Mister Rogers from A T & T here to see you," Kurtz announced.

The Admiral looked up from his desk and smiled.

"Admiral, could I have your audience for a few minutes?" Luther asked.

"Yes, of course." The Admiral made no attempt to rise, but instead, he shooed away the men as if what had been all-important was suddenly meaningless. The uniform clad men that had entered and exited without command ceased their indefatigable task. "What can I possibly do for the telephone business?"

"I'm not here representing AT&T. I am here to offer you my services."

The Admiral gave a suspecting glare as if Luther Rogers was trying to con him out of his family fortune. The old man before him was tall and thin, but not scrawny, he stood straight with a posture that Admiral Andrews admired. Blue veins and dark spots lined the hands that hung at his sides and his glasses were wire-rimmed teardrop bifocals. "Very well, what is it that I can do for you?" the Admiral asked.

Luther Rogers smiled. He noticed a picture of President Coolidge with his arm around the Admiral above the naval officer. He looked down at the man behind the desk, "I want to offer my boat and crew to help patrol the east coast against Nazi U-boats."

Admiral Andrews pushed himself back from the desk and again sized up the man who stood across from him. Luther Rogers was a man that gave off an aura of success and respect. Admiral Andrews knew the Cruising Club of America would start patrolling the east coast on anti-submarine picket duty March fourth. He hated the fact that his picayune forces had to incorporate civilian help but the son-of-a-bitch King, the chief-of-naval-operations, had obligated all the naval power to efforts in the Pacific.

"You're nearly eighty years-old. What do you think you could do against a German U-boat?" Admiral Andrews asked.

"Seventy-one," Luther replied. Admiral Andrews drove an axe into the tree of Luther Rogers. "I know I'm not young, but I have what it takes . . . determination. More than any teenager or young officer in your service."

"I'm sure you do, but I'm sorry. This war is for the young. I appreciate you taking the time to see me."

After that painful first rebuttal Luther Rogers redirected his cannons and unleashed the batteries. "Admiral, I didn't come up here to patronize you. So, please don't patronize me. I'm here to serve my country. To help protect the merchantmen who are dying within sight of our own shores. This isn't a war just for the young. This is a war to survive. I'm not going to sit idly by and watch the likes of you run our country into the hands of the Germans or Japanese. You might as well be killing those sailors yourself." Luther Rogers paused, turned his back to the admiral and faced the bookcase. He noticed a copy of Bowditch, paused, looked back with a disdainful glare at the Admiral, and then continued, "You are obviously not doing anything to save these young men. Last week I watched a ship burn off the New Jersey coast only a few miles from the beach. It's only been a few months since Pearl Harbor and we are now plunged into this damned war, all of us. The whole world is at war, more so than the Great War. I come to you with an offer of help and you can only mock me. This war is bigger than you and me. Look at you, you are long past being called young yourself. Every man has a right to protect his homeland. No, I take that back, an obligation." Luther took a breath. "Sir, I am going to go out there," he pointed, "and search for U-boats. I'll get a radio and call positions back to you whether you like it or not. We shall win this war despite fat pompous-asses like you who wish to ignore the goddamn enemy that's right under your nose."

"Mister Rogers, it is obvious you are very determined, and passionate. But, I am responsible for the protection of the east coast of the United States. You would be of no use out there chasing U-boats with no training, no equipment, and in a private yacht armed with only a wireless radio? My responsibility includes you too. You would simply be somebody else that I would have to worry about, a liability I sure as hell don't need right now. Be realistic," Admiral Andrews pleaded, ready to kick this pompous egotist out of his office.

Realistic was a word Luther Rogers left on the beach at Sandy Hook. "I wonder if the Poles, Czechs, or French would say that now? I know the British sure as hell are not realistic. You will regret this."

"I wish you well. Why don't you use your influence to raise war bonds? Or, help the country in some sort of capacity more suitable for a man of your maturity. Don't be a fool just because you saw some distant fire offshore."

Luther had already finished with this pig-headed bureaucrat. He nodded to the Admiral, said thank you and turned around, hoping he had the correct door.

He opened it and marched into a large office crowded with filing cabinets and steel desks, everyone in the room stopped and looked at the strange man in civilian clothes. Luther Rogers spotted an open doorway and then walked through the columns of paper toward the hallway. He recognized the waiting area and strode forward to retrieve his hat and overcoat. He gestured farewell with his hat to the receptionist and then exited.

Admiral Andrews sat at his desk, watching the man leave through the wrong door. Luther Rogers impressed him. Yes, with men like Luther Rogers they were going to win this war.

Five

He had not risen to sit on the board of the world's most powerful corporation by sitting idly by. Sending the Lincoln ahead, Luther decided to walk back to the brownstone. Reliving the confrontation in his mind, Luther became more disheartened and frustrated both at his age and the Coast Guard and Navy's stubbornness. Seventy-one years old, too damned old. I'm not old, he wanted to scream. As he walked down Broadway he saw a truck go past with Coopersmith painted on the wood side panel. He thought about the man he had seen at the club. The rumors, not that Luther paid much attention to such things, suggested that Coopersmith was connected to the mob with vast political associations. Luther thought back to the Admiral's reaction, dispensing with him because of his age infuriated and inspired him to fight that much more to overcome his age—he wasn't dead yet. Despite his position, most of Luther's political connections were long retired or dead. Maybe Coopersmith could help? Luther decided to take a chance and speak to the man. There was a brisk chill in the air, it felt like snow was on the way, it was revitalizing. Gripping his hat, he ran for a clearing in the traffic on 42nd street. He leaped for the curb and felt like running the entire way up to 44th but slowed and caught his breath instead.

The marble edifice looked like a library entrance, but it was not. The door man held the heavy oak open, "Good afternoon, Mister Rogers. Wonderful day today, feels like snow is coming."

"Thank you, Ed. I hope all is well in your life," Luther offered a quick salutation. He quickly hung his overcoat and homburg in the coatroom and strode through the foyer and into the sitting area. Luther scanned the expansive room, over-stuffed green velvet chairs paired up with cherry reading tables each with its own brass lamp were configured across the vast carpeted real estate. Tall thin windows allowed the late afternoon light to slice through the hovering cigar smoke. Deep carat paneled the walls. No pictures, bookshelves, seams, nothing broke the varnished interior with the exception of a marble hearth that had been converted to gas. Luther spotted the man he was after and briskly walked off the distance between them.

"Excuse me, Mister Coopersmith?" Luther Rogers asked the man behind a Wall Street Journal. He looked to be about fifty and his suit was tailored to show that he had not gone flabby over the years.

The man folded down the paper. A distinguished man dressed in a new single-breasted wool suit greeted him. Luther Rogers! Probably one of the most influential members of the New York Yacht Club! Despite the child-like awestruck enthusiasm, Harry Coopersmith knew how to handle situations like this— remain calm and unimpressed. He stood and reached out.

"Yes. To what do I owe this pleasure?"

"I am Luther Rogers. I was hoping you could help me."

Very direct, thought Harold Coopersmith. Something in the old man's expression radiated sincerity. "Well, how exactly may I help you?"

"Can we go somewhere private to talk?" Luther asked.

"After you, sir."

Luther led the man through the lounge of the New York Yacht Club. They walked passed portraits of long-ago commodores and record-breaking yachtsmen painted in oils, glass cases filled with trophies from every conceivable sailboat race from around the world, past the shrine embracing the America's Cup trophy and into a small room with only one long table surrounded by ten, high-backed, mahogany chairs— the race committee room.

"Are you in some sort of trouble Mister. . .ah. . ." Harry asked, pretending to forget this man's name—likely chance that would ever happen.

"Rogers. Please, Luther."

"Okay, Luther Rogers." Harold Coopersmith was accustomed to candor, but not in this place, after all this was the New York Yacht Club and Luther Rogers' face was on the wall with other past commodores. He had seen Luther Rogers at all the Club functions. He had wanted to meet the man who had won three Newport-Bermuda races, and held the world San Francisco-Tahiti record.

"Where shall I begin . . . With the war on . . . I went to Sandy Hook to see the tanker that was torpedoed last week and it struck me hard. The fact that the Nazi fleet is in the United States, in our waters, infuriates me. Frankly, it scares the hell out of me too." Luther Rogers paused and looked around the room. The walls were bare save for a chart of the Eastern Coast that decorated the far wall. He eyed the spot where the merchant ship had gone down. "I have to do something. The Navy is too busy in the Pacific. We're sitting ducks here. Our merchant fleet is being devastated." Luther paused for a moment to measure Coopersmith, see if he was still with him. Satisfied, he continued, choosing his words carefully, "I understand you have very influential friends and means to initiate certain unorthodox maneuvers without any bureaucratic entanglements."

Harold Coopersmith knew the old man was correct. He could avoid persecution in almost any state through ways of his own, but how did this man know? Not that it mattered, he loved it.

The man who looked at him with desperation in his eyes was a director on the board of the American Telephone and Telegraph Company, one of the world's largest companies. Harold was small time. Surely this man had access to money and political influences that he could only envy. "What is it you are asking of me, Mister Rogers?"

"I want to join the new Coast Guard Corsair Fleet. I have a sixty-five foot Hinckley that I want to use for anti-submarine patrol."

Harold felt a wave of relief cascade over his inflated ego. Admiral Andrew's East Coast defense arsenal hesitantly welcomed the Corsair Fleet—that collection of hastily assembled private yachts. It demonstrated the desperation of an unprepared nation to defend itself. The Corsair Fleet satisfied little in the way of anti-submarine warfare, nonetheless it was all that Andrews' could do in short notice to expand his need for an early warning system to protect the merchant fleet. Comprised of civilian boat owners inducted into the Coast Guard Reserve, the boats were armed with little more than a radio, and if lucky, surplus weapons and depth charges to perform picket duty against the German invasion.

He couldn't imagine why this man with so much to lose would want to risk his life to chase U-boats. Harold Coopersmith wanted nothing more than to profit from the war; he welcomed the Japanese bombing at Pearl Harbor. The capitalist possibilities were endless. In the few months since the United States induction into the war Harold Coopersmith had doubled his wealth, and saw himself walking away from the war a very, very rich man. With his new war-inspired confidence and economic bliss, Harry Coopersmith felt on top of the world. And now, one of the most powerful men in the country was at his doorstep begging him for help. The power!

"I can't promise anything. But, I'll try."

"That is all I ask of you. I do appreciate your efforts."

"Who do you have for a crew?" Harry expected to hear Ralph Hickman, Karl Miller, Chris Wells, or one of the other young racing crewmen that were currently representing the New York Yacht Club on the international racing circuit.

"Homer Crown," Luther replied.

"Homer Crown! You can't be serious. Does Homer still sail?"

"Mister Crown is one of the best sailors you'll ever see. He was the tactician on board the *Reliance*, and he has won more international races than any member alive, or dead."

"Reliance? When did she race?" Harry asked.

"She won the oh-three America's cup."

"Ah, I didn't mean to insult you."

"Nor I you."

"I'll see what can be done. It might be expensive," Harry said, leaving a pregnant pause in the air.

Luther Rogers acknowledged the last words and then stood and shook the hand of the man that would materialize his dream, his quest. He was growing from within. Luther Rogers felt the years fall away like autumn leaves and new green buds grow on his branches; that tree of fortitude once again grew outward, upward against the calling of the earth—death had hung over Luther Rogers like a shadow, but that shadow now receded in the glow of adventure.

Six

"What the hell did you go to that son-of-a-bitch for? He'd screw his own mother for a profit!"

"Calm yourself, Homer. We need people like him if we're going to get in the war and not sit back like two old geezers. Besides, he said he might be able to get us a position in the new Corsair Fleet."

"How?" Homer Crown asked with suspicion.

"I didn't ask. And, I don't care how Coopersmith is going to do it. As long as it gets us out there," Luther Rogers pointed toward the big bay window that offered a vista of water beating against a sandy beach. "I don't want to miss this."

Luther could never and would never admit that he was old, his mind was still as active as when he had been twenty. Nonetheless, he was afraid of getting too old to physically function. It was not death he feared; nor, was it the Nazis, it was his own ability that was being threatened by age that terrified him. And, now, he wanted to prove to the world that he could roar with the loudest of loins. That early morning on Sandy Hook, watching the tanker burn, aroused his spirit, a spirit that had been sinking lower into the stuffed leather chair behind his walnut desk. Luther Rogers wanted nothing more than to be catapulted into the war. His fortitude had issued the orders: save the young seamen of the merchant fleet. And, if it obliged his struggle with age, then even more so his resolution.

Homer agreed with Luther, he did not want to miss this. Homer thought back to the night in the water, watching the ship go down. He wanted revenge. He burned inside with the thought of not being able to tear into the chest of a Nazi and pull out the evil organ still pumping in his hands. The world was foolish to let a country that had been defeated by the combined efforts of the Allies only twenty years ago rise again to threaten all mankind. The insanity of it all!

"How soon did he say we could go?"

"Homer, there's a lot of things we have to do first. Put together a crew, but with everyone off to the recruiting stations that is going to be difficult. I suppose we have to be equipped with weapons that can sink a submarine; what kind of planning is there for sinking Nazis? I don't know. . . how do they track U-boats underwater? Hell, I don't even know if Coopersmith can even make this happen."

"Just follow the stench. The trail of the ruthless, murdering bastards can't be hard to find. Nonetheless, I don't feel at ease with the crook you've enlisted. I don't trust him."

"We don't have much choice. Let's start going over the things we might need. What about our affairs if we should not come back?" Luther knew that Homer was all too well acquainted with that unfortunate phenomenon.

"I've taken care of mine. I don't have anybody to leave it to. What about you?"

"My grandchildren can fight over it," Luther said, gazing out the window. He slowly turned to Homer, but was suddenly struck by a novel thought. "I'm going to will a considerable amount to the

Merchant Marines. There must be some organization that takes care of the welfare of those boys?"

"Marvelous idea, when should I submit your name for sainthood?" Homer asked him snidely. "What about weapons? Will we get a cannon? Will the boat hold a big gun? How do you shoot a U-boat?"

"Homer, slow down. We've got to get in the Corsair Fleet first. Want more coffee?" He asked walking to the walnut sideboard where a service tray sat loaded with the necessary condiments.

"No thanks. I read about depth charges. I hope we can get depth charges."

Caught up in the moment, Luther said, "I'm going to Darwrimple's to pick up the new set of heavy sails I ordered. I should refit the lines and tackle too. I would hate to have something break out there."

"I bet we could pick 'em off with a machine gun as they're running out of the hatches to get to their deck guns." Homer held an imaginary rifle in his hands, aimed at an imaginary German beast and pulled the imaginary trigger.

Looking at his watch, Luther saw the day was getting away from him. "Bernice is going to wonder what's happened to me. I'll leave you to your Germans and talk with you later when I get word back from Coopersmith." Luther Rogers left his friend shooting at imaginary U-boats. Walking down the wood steps, the sea breeze whipped his coat tails. Stepping into his Lincoln, Jimmy started it up, "Where to, sir?" Luther gazed out past the sand dunes at Long Island Sound, "Home, Jimmy." He thought back to his first war when he had been a young managing clerk at Union Station, not as busy as Grand Central, but for a twenty-seven year-old it was the most important job in the world. Telegrams began appearing from the far off Cuban front. The Spanish-American war was raging in the land just across the Florida Strait. Luther sat at his desk, mounted on a loft overlooking his responsibility of seven clerks, peering out the glass wall at the trains departing through the tunnel. He thought of leaving everything and joining the Army, but the few stories of savage acts on the Caribbean island, men losing their heads, being burned, flesh being notched away until death, the tales grew as they came North, and Luther Rogers, horrified of those exaggerated tales, did not go.

Living with his cowardice, Luther ascended the corporate ladder. Another war came along, this time on another island in the Pacific, and Luther, staring at the noon edition of the New York Times, fought an internal battle to sign-up. It was beginning of the new century and the Philippine War was raging in humid jungles of the Pacific, he wavered, vacillating to go or remain at his secure position with Bell Telephone. Finally, despite the pleas of his wife, Bernice, he went to the recruiting station down on 32nd street. The Army was not looking for any immediate recruits; their budget would not allow it. Luther thought it an omen and withdrew his original request for adventure. Still, he felt cheated out of his chance to test his manhood; a juvenile premise to an age-old ideation of verifying one's bravery. Time brought another opportunity: the Great War in Europe. Luther fantasized about going to Europe and fighting for the British or French. By that time he was married with two children, and could not join—the early notions of testing himself were, he realized, a childish penchant—he waved the troops off with secret envy.

Luther saw the evidence of war. He often walked nostalgically past his old office in the train station—the loading platform was a courier of history. The United States finally entered the war to end all wars. Luther wanted to join the passengers that wore on their faces the scars of experience that he could read, not touch. By nineteen seventeen the Great War raged and his children were gone and Bernice was not as dependent on him as she had once been. Luther went to the recruiter and was denied the honor of serving his country; moreover, he was denied the ability to test his character. Luther Rogers lived with the torment, longing to test his courage on the field of battle. He knew not the carnage and gruesomeness of the battlefield but at forty-six he was too old to fight.

His mind came back to the present day as Jimmy brought the car to a stop. Excitement built in his chest as he climbed the brick steps of the brownstone and entered through the thick oak doors. Luther wrapped his arms around Bernice and kissed the back of her neck. "There you are. I'm glad you're back. Your granddaughter is coming by for dinner. She just finished up winter exams. She's bringing a friend over."

Luther grabbed a carrot from the cutting board and stepped back. "Is Louise bringing what's his name, Mike or something?" Luther asked, chomping on the carrot.

Bernice used the back of her hand while holding the knife to push back a gray strand of hair. "No, she hasn't dated him in almost a year. Besides, I think he joined up. No, she's bringing Sue." Bernice turned back to her culinary chores, "You remember Sue. She came out to the summer house last August."

Luther grunted an acknowledgement and retreated to the study. He had to write a letter to the shipyard to get the Hinckley in before she entered service. 'Service', Luther smiled at the thought of a shiny new coat of blue on the freeboard, sailing at battle stations.

Seven

Homer Crown thought of Gary Cooper in Sergeant York. He pictured himself taking five or six U-boats on a single patrol. He would come back into the harbor with hundreds of dead Nazis piled on the decks. A bell rang as he pushed open the glass door. The small gun shop was dark except for the soft glow of afternoon light coming in through the entrance. The rows of rifles and shotguns stood at attention in the shadows behind a glass counter top, wood racks held more long guns forming aisles. Homer felt a sense of power rush in with his breath from the sight of such an armory. With the hunch of age in his posture, as if he was falling face-first, Homer walked to the counter with the momentum of gravity propelling him forward.

"Good mornin', what kin I do fer ya?" a voice said from beyond the columns of blue barrels. A small man with a pouch that hung over what must have been his belt buckle appeared from among the rows of rifles and took his place behind the counter, resting his elbow on the top of an old hand-crank register. Homer noticed the .38 revolver that hung on the man's side.

"I want a Springfield oh-three rifle."

"A rifle . . . whadda ya gonna do? Hunt, krauts?" The shop owner laughed at his own joke.

"Yes," Homer said.

The forceful, no-nonsense rebuttal left the shop owner absent of a witty comeback. He looked at the old man with a discerning eye. He was taller by a few inches but with a permanent slouch as if he were lighting a cigarette in the wind, the old man could've been five ten or eleven in his youth. The man who wanted to kill krauts must be seven hundred years old, the shop owner thought.

"Yer serious, ain't ya mista?" The shop owner didn't wait for a reply, and Homer Crown wasn't giving any. "Well, the oh-three is a good rifle . . . If'in yer gonna kill someone though, I think a faster

46

rifle mightin' be a sight better." Homer followed the shop owner through the maze of shelves and gun racks. He stopped to face the back wall. The shop owner paused, scanned the row of rifles and spotted the one he wanted to sell the old man. "This here's the one fer you. Let me git it fer ya. Now this is a new auto-loading repeater. A semi-auto. Takes an H an' H three seventy-five magnum round. It's built by a small gun company upstate, Ithaca. It'll hold nine rounds and one in the chamber."

"It's very light," Homer said, hoisting the weapon in his hands to judge the weight.

"Yes, they use an exotic jungle wood of some such. I can't recall what they call it. It'll put holes in a kraut at five hundred yards," The man claimed.

"I can't see that far. But, I'll take it." Homer said.

They walked back to the glass counter. The shop owner let Homer carry the weapon. "I want five hundred rounds for it and how much is that revolver there?"

"That one?" the owner looked down through the glass top.

"Yes, that one."

"You huntin' bear too? That there's a four fifty-four Colt. It'll blow holes the size of pie plates through dem krauts. Want that, too? I'll wrap 'er. A course y'ill need two hundred rounds fer 'er."

Homer wrote out a check for the weapons and ammunition. "Could you have all of it delivered to this address," Homer asked, handing over the check and his calling card.

"Yes I can. Have a good day, sir." The shop owner said, clearly ecstatic about the sale.

Homer stepped out onto the sidewalk and gazed up at an over-cast sky and opened his mouth as if to catch rain drops. He felt for his leather cigar case and pulled out a Tampa hand-rolled cigar. He withdrew his watch chain, finding the cigar punch at the end of the fob Homer drilled the end of the tobacco. Satisfied, he lit the corona with a gold pocket lighter and then took in a mouthful of smoke, savoring the flavor. He turned back to the shop before walking to the taxi and saw a reflection of an old man in the storefront window. Who is that man and what the hell was he doing? There had never been a firearm in his life. His father, an Episcopal minister in White Plains, had never allowed a gun in the house. Homer did not give his father's convictions much thought when growing up, not interested in guns, his interests focused on sailing. The minster gave his son a dinghy sailboat when Homer was only eight years old. He took to sailing like a fish to water and soon competed in local sailboat races where boys raced almost anything powered by sail. The local yacht club welcomed the minister's ten-year-old son for his capabilities—on the Hudson River he reigned undefeated for the entire summer. Robert Gannet invited the young sailor to join the crew on his George Steers six-meter racer and it was only after one and half seasons that Homer graduated to tactician. Gannet started winning races and soon was invited to the New York Yacht Club to race with thirteen-year-old Homer Crown as his tactician on board the Herreshoff fin keel sloop. With no formal training Homer exhibited a natural instinct for gauging the wind and the ability to react instantly with the proper sail trim to gain the most speed possible, it was a gift from God as his father said to him.

While attending college Homer started selling tack for horse racing in hopes of buying his own sailboat. The small company did well and Homer quit college to focus more energy on building the business. When he had enough capitol Homer bought a company that fabricated metal products for horse wagons. In two short years he restructured and expanded the business ten-fold. No longer did he make horse cart parts, but office cabinets, metal furniture hardware, typewriter housings, bicycle frames, and railroad car fixtures. Homer sold the company for $12 million in 1896 when he was only twenty-nine and thus began a life concentrated on becoming the most celebrated yachtsman in the world; and, that is exactly what he did.

Homer threw down the soggy cigar butt and crushed it with his shoe. He thought of the rifle and that Colt revolver, the Nazis were dead men.

Eight

At night the ocean became a black void.

The shadows and reflections that danced on the surface could not penetrate into the dark kingdom below. An active imagination created three-headed serpents and huge monsters, gliding just beneath the surface. That is what Seaman Mead did as he watched a strange creature race toward the ship. He had been on lookout watch for twenty minutes.

The full moon made the ocean surface come alive with brilliance. Each passing wave that broke the line of reflected light from the moon's illumination was some horrible creature, a U-boat, a German warship, no, a lifeboat from a downed ship. Yes, that's what it is! A lifeboat.

Mead strained to see the shadow that was taking shape, a silhouette of a boat. It was dead in the water, floating still. Mead saw a line of brightness in the water down on the port side—a flash of phosphorescent plankton came alive.

Then, he heard a dull thump, originating from the bottom of the earth as if the ship had just run aground. The ship vibrated. Suddenly, another tail of glowing microorganisms appeared. Seaman Mead studied the mysterious light; another appeared. Again, there was a tremendous reverberation sent through the ship's hull. The third hit was not a dull knock but a colossal blast that sent flames soaring into the night. The ship split in two like a fragile glass and disappeared into the inky-black void beneath the surface.

Kapitanleutnant Fulmer, commanding officer of *Unterseebot-251*, lowered his binoculars. He had not expected such a brilliant display. What had been a roaring splendor of red, yellow and orange that reached with out-stretched arms toward the heavens was now a vacancy in the ocean's darkness.

He scanned quickly for survivors, finding none he ordered the U-boat north. He must vacate the area in the event a destroyer nearby. To date he heard not a single word of a German Imperial Navy *Unterseeboot* being lost in the happy hunting ground off the American East Coast. It was a phenomenon that the Admiralty exploited with great affect and propagandized with equal enthusiasm, but like most Kapitans he knew his luck could not hold out forever. The Americans would fight back soon—astonishing that they had not put more effort in stopping him and his fellow U-boat comrades in their effort of devastating the United States shipping routes. He did not want to be the first to feel the wrath of this young nation. He wanted to return home with every torpedo expended into the side of an American freighter, Ursula would be so proud of him. He would get the Iron Cross.

The beast's bow cut through the inky surface. The blackness beneath was no mystery to the steel monster. It was his leviathan that appeared out of the depths, anywhere, anytime, undetected, unannounced that gave Fulmer the sensation of power. He drove one of the most advanced war machines in the world. The U-boat was not a guest floating on the top of its host, like the large ships that traveled the oceans, but instead, the U-boat melded together with the ocean, it became apart of the black void. As far as the world and the ignorant Americans were concerned, like the shark, there were no predators for the U-boat—it roamed the waters unchallenged to leave a wake of destruction. Not in the entire United States maritime history has such a devastating blow against shipping been suffered—most of the causalities suffered within sight of the east coast shore.

Nine

Harry Coopersmith left the club early. He thought about his meeting with Luther Rogers. He really had made it, Luther Rogers coming to him for favors! The scent of flowers caught his attention, a street vendor displayed four terraced rows of flower bouquets despite the late winter season. "Give me that bouquet there," Harry told the vendor. He reached into his pocket and pulled out his gold money clip, peeling off a five he handed it to the man, "Keep the change." He felt like he had won a stakes race at Belmont. Although the sky was gray and overcast the sun shone in Harry's mind. Harry flagged down a taxi, jumped in, and barked out his Yonkers address. The taxi fought to get out into the Manhattan traffic, but slowly it inched its way north through the maze of taxis and buses and north-bound vehicles and soon they made their way across the river to the burgeoning suburbs. The more he thought about someone of Luther Rogers' stature in corporate America—the legitimate world unmolested by having to deal with the nefarious sort Harry was forced to conduct business with to succeed in his profession—the more his smile grew. The smile showed on his face and throughout his body. Harry knew that this day would be remembered as the day that Harry Coopersmith reached the absolute pinnacle of success. He had a bounce in his step as he walked up the sidewalk to his Leighton Avenue home. He couldn't wait to tell Patty his story. Although he was a ruthless businessman skirting the law, Harry had an undying love and attraction for his wife. Quietly he eased the storm door to the back entrance, stopping momentarily like a cat burglar as the hinges squeaked. He continued slowly, opening the heavy door and walked in through the kitchen to find his wife already there.

"Harry, why are you using the servants' entrance?" Patty asked, but smiled when she saw the flowers, "for me?"

"Yes, for you my beautiful wife," Harry said, following her into the dinning room.

Patty had been a svelte young student when Harry first met her at Saratoga racetrack. Although she had put on weight over the years, it was well proportioned and only added to his attraction. He still saw the gorgeous college student he fell in love with just before the first big war. They had married in a small chapel on the Penn Yan Women's College campus. Soon after the wedding the United States entered the European conflict and his economic life changed as well as his domestic one. Harry served as a quartermaster in the Army stateside during the Great War in a billet that allowed him sufficient time to keep his trucking business going. The black market wasn't in huge demand back then, but what little call there was for government products Harry Coopersmith quietly sold on the side, making him a small sum. However, during that Great War, the fortune was in relationships with people that existed on the fringe of society. He established himself as a trusted teamster for the up and coming bootleggers during prohibition. Eventually, the daily produce runs to the city from the Upstate farms turned to booze from Canada. Harry hated to replace his trusted Belgium teams with gasoline-powered trucks, but he was smart enough to recognize the advantages. When the business was lucrative enough he started to buy thoroughbreds. Again his moral compass pointed toward the criminal population in horse racing. It wasn't that Harry wanted to venture into the criminal world, or even be a part of it, it was simply that the organized criminal network and corrupt politicians were the prevalent controlling body over that industry. Harry Coopersmith loved horses ever since he was a young child working with his dad's team of grey spotted draft horses. It was a passion, a love for those graceful and powerful creatures that stayed with him. Surprising even Harry, horse racing thrived during the depression. It appeared that Harry had the Midas touch and his wealth grew even during the leanest years of the economic onslaught of the thirties. He purchased a small fledgling track in the Catskill Mountains and built it up as a prestigious place to summer with nearby resorts that brought vaudeville entertainers from the city to perform. Soon the Catskills were the place to go for honeymoons, weekend getaways, and family vacations, especially for those of the population that did not summer in their mansions on Long Island.

Patty stood arranging the flowers on the dining room table. Harry sat on one of the chairs admiring his wife's perfect beauty. "You'll never guess who came to see me today?"

"Santa Claus?" Patty said, stepping back to evaluate her arrangement.

"Luther Rogers of A, T and T," he said trying to impress her.

"Sonia, would you please get me a Darjeeling tea and a coffee for Mister Coopersmith, thank you." Patty sat across from her husband. "So what did Luther Rogers of A, T and T want with Harold Coopersmith of Coopersmith Incorporated?"

He smiled at her mocking. "He wants me to help him get in the war."

Her eyebrows drew together in thought, Harry never got sick of looking into those blue eyes and even after twenty-five years of staring into that beautiful face he was still smitten. "How can you possibly get him in the war? Couldn't he just go enlist like everyone else?" Patty asked.

Harry reclined as Sonia set down a silver, engraved tray and disappeared back into the kitchen. "He's about seventy-five years old. He wants to take his yacht out and sink German U-boats."

"U-boats, Germans have U-boats? What's a U-boat?" She asked, stirring honey into her tea.

"Submarines, or whatever the Huns call them. I am shocked that this man, who is undoubtedly one of the most powerful men in the country, is coming to me for assistance."

Patty reached out and touched her husband's hand lightly. Her blue eyes looked into him. "You are one of the most powerful men in the country, Harry. You should realize that because Luther Rogers of A, T and T came to you. How are you going to do it?"

"I could go see Richardson, he owes me a favor or two."

Patty shook her head. "No, I would go see Vinnie Costa first. It would help develop your relationship with him, make him feel important. Besides, he probably would think it quite patriotic. He loves this patriotic sentiment that has overtaken the country since Pearl Harbor."

"I suppose you're right. I'll see how that goes, but boy to be able to help Luther Rogers!"

The next day Harry stopped by the office to check on the daily machinations of his empire before heading off to Costa's. He drove himself in the Packard, although he hated to drive in Manhattan he wanted the flexibility and with the elation and excitement he felt he was too anxious to wait for a taxi.

"Coopersmith here to see you, sir," Costa's secretary announced through the office intercom.

"Send him in!" A voice called back through the brown box that sat on the secretary's desk.

Harry walked into the immense, intimidating office of the most powerful man he knew. He wondered for the first time if there was a scale to measure power where did Luther Rogers rate on that scale. His feet slid sideways as the weight of each step fell into the plush blood-red carpet. Bookshelves burdened with hundreds of law books made up most of the décor. A brass rail ran along the middle of the bookshelves and ended at a glass bar on the far side. Two oak frames hung above the scotch, gin, soda water, and tonic: one, a picture of a thoroughbred Harry recognized as the winning horse, Cullion, he had sold Vinnie eight years ago, and the other, a Daily News headline, "PHARLAP DEAD." Harry wondered if Vinnie had been the one behind the murder of the greatest racehorse to ever live.

It was a full ten steps to the chair that was offered him. The view through the glass that stretched behind Vinnie from corner to corner grew as Harry approached, it must be thirty-five feet of window he guessed. It was said that Vincent Costa needed such a view to survey his empire. Down there, in the spires of concrete, steel, and asphalt, was the Mayor's office, One Police Plaza, the Federal building, all of New York.

"Harry, so glad to see you. You look great."

"Hello, Mister Costa. You're as fit as ever."

"What's with the 'Mister' crap, I'm Vinnie to you! What brings you my old friend another horse for sale?"

"I'm here to ask for your advice," Harry said.

Vinnie bowed his balding head, indicating that he would listen and offer any advise he could, and then stretched in his high-back leather chair and offered his full mental capacity. He was a man who possessed all the finest virtues of character, but also, he possessed some of the worst. What made Vincent Costa powerful was his ability to select the best trait for any given occasion. So, now, he listened with the greatest sincerity.

"I have been approached by a very rich man. This rich man wants to join the Corsair picket fleet the Coast Guard is organizing. He would pay and probably do anything to get involved."

"Why can't he volunteer like everyone else?"

"Too old."

"And, you want me to get him in the Coast Guard? Well, that's easy. It's a good thing, those damn U-boats are causing hell with my freighters. You don't realize the problem. I've got money tied up in boats that can't leave port and, if they do . . . sometimes they don't make it. I just lost a freighter that had seven hundred-fifty thousand dollars of goods aboard." Vincent Costa was frustrated. He had found an enemy he couldn't buy, nor intimidate. "Consider it done. This is one thing I would be proud to do, help kill those lousy Nazi and Jap bastards"

"Claire, get me Senator Wagner on the telephone." Costa released the intercom button and turned to lift the lid of the ornate Brazilian wood humidor on his desk Vinnie withdrew a cigar from it and offered Harry one. Harry shook his head, "No thank you." After cutting the end with a guillotine and lighting it with a kerosene desktop torch, Vinnie exhaled the blue-gray smoke.

Claire's voice on the intercom announced that the Senator was waiting on the line. Vinnie offered a mischievous grin to Harry as he picked up the receiver.

"Bob, how are you today."

Harry could only hear Vinnie's side of the conversation. Nonetheless, he was impressed with the casualness of his demeanor toward United States Senator Robert Wagner. Hell, the New York Senator was part of Roosevelt's brain trust.

"Listen, I need you to get someone into the Coast Guard's Corsair Fleet." Vinnie cupped the telephone and asked Harry, "What's his name?"

"Rogers, Luther Rogers." Harry scooted to the front of his chair with excitement. "And his boat. Tell him to commission his boat, too," Harry whispered to Vinnie.

"Luther Rogers and his boat. Yes, that Luther Rogers. I don't know. I appreciate it, Bob. I'll have Claire send over a box of those Cubans cigars you like."

Proud of himself, Vinnie showed his straight yellow teeth as he set the receiver back down in its cradle. "I've got him wrapped around my little finger. Said it'd be no problem." Luther Rogers, eh? He used to be something in this town, when he was Theodore Vail's right hand man and President at A, T & T. Now there is some real power. It seems like every year they're making leaps-and-bounds, telephone calls across the country, across the Atlantic, and now even across the Pacific. When will it end?" Vinnie looked into Harry's brown eyes and said, "Harry this is my gift to you. You're going to gain quite a bit of influence with this old geezer." Harry didn't need to be told, but now he owed a small favor to Vincent Costa, a favor he was glad to pay.

Vinnie switched tracks, blowing smoke into the ceiling fan, "How is the racing business?"

"The track is booming. I haven't seen such turn-outs since twenty-nine." The thoroughbred racing industry had prospered throughout the depression, but the war had given people paychecks, and for the first time during war, the cavalry did not need horses. Horse racing was in its most opulent hour. Harry's New York and Louisiana tracks were experiencing the best returns in memory.

"Next Wednesday I want to bring your boy, Michael, up to the house in the hills for a party. Is he still at Princeton?" Vinnie said.

"Yes, he is."

"Tell Michael, when he gets done with school he'll have a good decent job waiting for him."

"Thank you, Michael will be delighted."

"I wish I were young again." Vinnie laughed, "I'd be screwin' all them co-eds. Michael must be having a hell-of-a good time. Make sure to give him my invitation."

Harry departed Costa's office, past Claire who rode lead over the small staff of office workers. That was easier than expected, Patty was right as usual, Costa loved this patriotic bullshit that spread across the country. As long as horse racing and trucking were still needed he would wave a flag too. Hell, the war was filling the gates at the track and the need to get supplies from the industrial Midwest to the ports on the coast was never as lucrative. Harry hoped the war would last a long, long time.

Ten

Maxwell Jackson, Sonarman Second Class, sat in the crews lounge on the *Coast Guard Cutter Spencer*. Max stretched his legs out across the desk, his waist disappeared in the uniform. A stocky man sat opposite him. "Jackson, let's volunteer for the landing craft operations. The message said they're looking for Coast Guard Coxswains to take Marines ashore. We'll drive right up to the front door of the Emperor's palace in Japan."

Max sat up. "I could go for that. Sure would beat this old bucket. The Pacific, naked girls. We could show them rice-eaters a thing or two. Are you serious?"

Munro had that look in his eye that meant he was. Max had seen that same face when they had painted 'W' (the recognition letter preceding all Coast Guard hull numbers) on the hull numbers to USS Niagara. They were tied-up in

Boston, the crews of both ships were practicing the age-old art of tormenting each other. Six crewmembers from the Niagara sat in the far table of the Wildwind, catching a glimpse of the Coast Guardsmen. They called over, "How many Coasties does it take to bury their dead at sea?"

"How many?" Two voices asked out in unison.

"Three, two to hold 'em up and one to pound him into the mud."

"How come Coasties have to be six feet or taller?"

A thin sailor played along, "Why?"

"Because when their boats sink they can walk ashore." The group broke out into laughter.

Munro yelled out a rebuttal, "Yeah, swab-jockeys don't have to worry about it. Shit floats." The Coasties became hysterical. It was later that night that Munro, his eyes seething with conviction, persuaded his band of Coast Guard-commandos. The mission had gone well, even in the frigid Boston Harbor water. They swam to the Niagara pushing paint cans and brushes on a makeshift raft and had spent the night, drunk with silliness, painting the Coast Guard "W" on the hull numbers that were high on the freeboard and transom, but that was long before Pearl Harbor.

Munro, with the same piercing conviction in his eyes, stood up and slammed down the three month-old Saturday Evening Post. "Yes. If you're not serious about it . . . just stay and rot. I want to see some action."

Max joined the Coast Guard for adventure and this was his chance. "Think they would let us shoot some Japs? Just imagine storming in toward the shore. Bombs going off everywhere. Bullets flying. It'd be great. We'd be right in the heat of it all."

"Yeah, the Marines would go charging up into cover and we'd have to go back and get another load. Never out of sight of the machine guns." Munro was truly adamant. "The Marines would love us. The swab-jockeys would envy us. We'd be heroes!"

Both of the young Guardsmen marched up to the ship's clerk and filled out the request for transfer forms. It was anticlimactic. They signed papers that an expressionless yeoman proffered and the fantastical adventures of gunfire, bombs, and dead Japs was translated into long forms in triplicate. They envisioned a grand parade of congratulations and exaltations for volunteering but instead the yeoman, a prematurely balding man from Iowa, handed them another triplicate request form—the slow transfer process began.

Max went through his daily routine aboard, his mind filled with the grandeur of rushing in toward the beach, defying the enemy's marksmen—the daydreamer of glory on the beachhead. The admin officer, Lieutenant Stallings, asked both eager transferees if either could sail, as in a sailboat. Munro asked in reply, "What does that have to do with killing Japs and driving Marines to the beach, sir?"

"I don't know, Munro. Apparently, someone is looking for a blow-boater."

"Growing up I sailed with my brother at Boy Scout camp," Max answered, thinking nothing of it. Then, as suddenly as Munro had launched the idea in his mindset, orders appeared for both eager guardsmen. Munro received transfer orders to the Navy as signalman for small boat operations, he was ecstatic. Jackson read his orders to report to Brooklyn Navy Yard for assignment aboard the *CGR65320*. Max was a little confused. Did the Coast Guard have landing craft already? The *CGR65320* meant it was a sixty-five foot Coast Guard vessel, in Brooklyn? Was he going to Europe! And, fight Hitler! He read on . . .Corsair fleet! What the hell was the Corsair fleet? That must mean that Max was going to Europe to fight. Munro looked over Max's shoulder at the orders with envy.

"Not good, Jackson? You might be the luckiest of all. I'll probably end up dead on some beach while you're getting lucky with all the women in Paris, you lucky dog."

Max tried to smile. "I don't feel so lucky. I thought we'd stick together and chase grass-skirted, bare-chested dames on tropical islands."

Munro put his arm around his friend's shoulder. "Maybe you can sink a U-boat."

Munro and Max both knew that a landing craft could not sink a German U-boat, anymore than man could walk on the moon. It took the technology, speed, and armament of a destroyer to sink a U-boat. The whole idea of the Corsair Fleet was foreign to them. It must be some special operation against the Nazi war machine. Max gave a half-hearted congratulation to Munro and went below to pack his things. The war suddenly got real. The thought of proceeding alone to face the Nazis scared the shit out of him. He should have never put in for that transfer. The doubt and incertitude seeped into his thoughts like a leaky faucet, and soon overwhelming consternation overflowed. Max felt like he was being sent to the executioner's block, he'd miss the camaraderie in *Spencer*. He would have been better off if he had never listened to Munro, then he wouldn't be leaving the cutter for something strange and unwelcome or worse a lonely death on some European beach.

His orders came complete with a set of instructions in the manila colored envelope. He loaded his sea bag on the train and read as he made his way south. He was being put into very unusual circumstances. He had to train the entire crew of *CGR65320* and he was to be the executive officer, XO! It was a hollow consolation for being yanked from the comfort and familiarity of the cutter.

Eleven

Harry Coopersmith entered the marina in West Egg about four-thirty in the afternoon. The sky was already looking forward to night. Vinnie Costa had called Harry earlier that day with instructions to pass along to the new Coast Guardsmen and shortly afterward an ensign from the Navy Department had called Harry with information for Luther Rogers and news about a refit for his yacht—the sailboat needed to be reconfigured for war at the Brooklyn Navy Yard. Harry walked along the dock, a few yachts occupied the finger piers but most slips were empty as the boats were laid up for the winter. The boy at the entrance said that Mister Rogers was on his boat, slip sixty-one. Harry would have admired the sailboats that lined the dock, but today he was too excited about the news, his ability, his influence and power! He felt the urge to run. He walked conscious of every step in order to restrain his stride so it wouldn't surge forward out of control.

"Mister Rogers? Anybody aboard?" He called out to the yacht.

Luther Rogers appeared from out of the hatch. He pulled on a wool coat as the air starting to turn cold with the approaching darkness. "Hello, Mister Coopersmith. How'd you find me?"

He gave an expression that said 'I'm all powerful, nothing is out of my grasp' but offered no verbal reply.

"What are you here for? Any news?"

"Yes, you are to have this boat over to the Brooklyn Navy Yard by tomorrow morning. They're going to fit it with weapons. And then move it to a mooring in Long Beach at Point Lookout. Closer to the action I suppose."

"My God, I don't believe it!" Luther Rogers couldn't hide his excitement, he grinned like a boy. "You really did it. Phenomenal! It's hard to believe. I thought it'd take months, but you did it in three days!" Luther shook his hand vigorously.

"I am a man never to be underestimated."

"So, indeed." Luther could see the glow, the self-admiring color in Harry's face. He didn't care, Harry had done it. "Join me below."

Luther Rogers entered the cabin and retrieved a bottle of 1931 Moet. He held out two flutes, popped the cork, filled them and handed one to Harry. "To your and my success."

Harry touched Luther's glass then swallowed the entire contents. Luther wanted to hug the man. He began pouring him another but Harry pulled his glass back. "No, I must be off. I am a man who can not idle around on sailboats."

"Thank you, Mister Coopersmith. What do I owe you for this?"

"You can call it my patriotic duty. Remember me, Luther, just remember me," Harry said.

"I'll do more than that, Harry. I will rejoice in your name," Luther said, slapping Harry on the back with enthusiasm as he guided him out of the Hinckley. Harry smiled with satisfaction and then strode back to his waiting red

Packard with even more satisfaction.

Twelve

Brooklyn, a borough predominantly residential, was covered with buildings that seldom exceeded twenty stories—a sprawling forest of brick and concrete and asphalt in the shadow of Manhattan. Dodgers Stadium dominated the landscape and the mood of the borough celebrated with pride for their baseball team, however it was the Navy Yard that occupied a vast majority of the Brooklyn waterfront that provided the city's stipend. Cranes, with hooks and baskets dangling, soared above the rows of warehouses and drydocks, the yard was compact yet vast. Luther and Homer sailed the Hinckley— polished and decorated with new tackle and sails—into the mouth of the busy shipbuilding institution. The dark blue freeboard reflected the Manhattan skyline on the port and Brooklyn's industrial view on the starboard. A dockmaster stood at the pier with a cigarette dangling from his lips. He motioned Luther to moor along the seawall, under the neck of a crane that looked like a stork waiting to pick up a young baby. Somehow the dockmaster was able to communicate with Luther without losing the Camel, "Just put 'er right here. Hand me that line."

Luther complied, throwing the bowline up to the Camel. Homer Crown grabbed a piling to keep the stern in. The dockmaster came back and received the stern line from Homer. Unceremoniously, they were moored. "Out you two. We've got work to do—special orders. You two the only crew?" The dockmaster didn't wait for a reply but instead walked off, barking orders at his gang of workers. The yard workers, tough looking rogues too dirty to touch the pristine yacht, ran straps under the hull—one forward and one aft and then quickly hoisted the sailboat onto a cradle in an empty corner of the yard. Three more men applied their trade, shoring-up the yacht into position, moving a scaffold into position, and rolling in heavy equipment Luther did not recognize. Luther Rogers watched in disbelief at the speedy transition of his race boat. The dockmaster strode toward them and said, "You two are going to have to get out of here, we got work to do and I don't need a couple of old geezers in my way." Luther and Harry, their excitement deflated by the unceremonious turnover, headed toward Jimmy in the waiting Lincoln.

Luther and Homer devoted a portion of their days to visit the Hinckley to observe the conversion from racing yacht to a machine of war. The Navy Yard was a human beehive of welders, riveters, carpenters, stevedores, all the clamor of a Navy hurrying to meet the demands of a world war. Luther Rogers did not notice the noise because he was too overcome with the rapidity and unceremonious attention his Hinckley received. In just two quick days since Homer and Luther first sailed into this industrial behemoth the yard workers transformed it into a vessel of war. He had arrived two days ago full of sagacity—his vision of fresh gleaming freeboards was tainted by the ugly grey paint that covered the most beautiful yacht afloat. The once sleek hull that blazed through the water with glistening dark blue hull, spotless burnished teak, and glossy white superstructure, now sat, cradled in worn timber and rusted supports, hid beneath a dull ageless blandness. Somehow, Luther had thought that *Lady* would glide silent through the sea in all her brilliance and color and blow Nazi U-boats clean out of the water. Nonetheless, he conceded the practicality of the new hide.

Luther held a can of black paint in his left hand, in his right was a small brush that was following the curve in "R." The new name came from something deep down inside, a sensation stronger than the added adjective, a battle cry from all the drowned sailors. Luther stepped back to admire the new moniker. He looked out at the harbor, past Governors Island: a woman was standing erect, with the certitude of a nation. She held her flame up high toward heaven as if telling the people that she was on guard screaming, "Follow me." That lady possessed an unequivocal resolve, she could welcome many people from far-off lands, comfort the downtrodden, remain steadfast against changing political winds, reinstate a country's values, but most of all, inspire the fight for freedom. Luther had never considered himself an overt patriot, even now his proclivities were somewhat tainted with self-edification, he was a business man, but today, and for the rest of this war, he was a man resolved to uphold the beliefs that had once formed this nation. The Statue of Liberty seemed to smile at him.

Luther Rogers examined his artwork with satisfaction.

"*Lady's Revenge*, a fitting name Mister Rogers. I thought it was bad luck to change the name of a boat."

Luther Rogers spun around startled. He smiled at the stalker.

"My name's Petty Officer Jackson, at your service."

"Hello, Petty Officer Jackson. I don't believe in all that sailor superstition. Are you with the yard?" Luther asked, noticing the uniform.

"Hell no, I ain't no swab-jockey. I'm a Coast Guardsman. Hasn't anyone talked to you? The oh-oh-dee said you were Mister Rogers, captain of the *CGR65320*. I am your XO."

"I am . . .but no one called me about an executive assistant."

"I'm not an executive assistant, I'm your executive officer, second in command," Max explained to the civilian. It reaffirmed his disgust at the new assignment. Max wanted to go to the Pacific and drop Marines on the beach. He wanted to be in the action. While Munro would be off saving the world, Maxwell Jackson would be babysitting a geriatric boat. This crew needed a nursemaid not a Sonarman in the United States Coast Guard. The only thing that kept the twenty-one-year-old petty officer from commenting on his assignment aloud was his military discipline.

"Sir, I have been assigned to this vessel. I am to act as executive and weapons officer aboard this . . ." Max surveyed the grey hull, "thing."

"What? Really? I don't know what to say? I suppose I should be pleased to have a young fighting man aboard. And, I am pleased." Luther Rogers was relieved yet disappointed. He had a weapons expert and someone who would know how to sink a U-boat, but the boy didn't look old enough to drive an automobile let alone fight a war. Not his kind of war.

The mysterious underwater craft were elusive and they would need a person with the education to combat this strange foe. Luther Rogers was disappointed, no absolutely dumbfounded at the lack of training the Navy, or Coast Guard, that was now a part of the Navy, offered to the Corsair Fleet. It was as if the Navy said, 'Got a boat? Good. Here's some depth charges now go sink a U-boat. They're out there." When Harry Coopersmith provided him this extraordinary opportunity Luther felt like a wanton seed waiting to grow, the dirt was *Lady's Revenge*, sunlight was the conviction to help those helpless merchant mariners, and Harold Coopersmith poured the water. His convictions grew to a sapling, then, rose to a hundred foot redwood. Luther Rogers wanted more than anything in his life to feel that vigor and juvenile bliss of being on guard, protecting his nation, contributing in some meaningful way to the cause. His confidence had been shrinking each day the Navy yard put a new weapon on board without the slightest hint of how to work the damn thing. First came the water-cooled machine gun, contractors stormed aboard with power drills and then cut and bolted the thing into place. Luther winced as the men bore into the deck of his beautiful Hinckley. They screwed a bracket to the foc's'l and mounted the odd looking gun, the barrel was twenty times the diameter of the bore with a small funnel where the front sights should be. The green tripod was bolted through the teak deck and white caulk was piled around the base of each leg to prevent leaks into the cabin. Then, without remorse, the yard workers tore apart the stern of the boat, first they removed the lifelines and travel-all across the transom leaving only the flagstaff, and then two ugly, maladroit steel framed apparatus' were fastened to port and starboard. Down below an air compressor was installed, its umbilical of high pressure air was run up through a hole drilled in the teak and attached to the repulsive racks on the stern.

"What are you trained to do?" Luther asked, his mind returning to the young man standing next to him.

"My rate, that's what they call your specialty training, is sonar."

Luther Rogers didn't know whether to be delighted or disappointed, knowing his second-in-command was a sonar specialist. "What does . . .what is sonar?"

"I didn't know either when I went to school. But after a while it grows on you. SONAR stands for sound navigation and ranging."

"You're a navigator?"

"No, a sub-killer. Sonar is what we use to detect submarines, or U-boats underwater. Like an underwater microphone, it can listen or ping and wait for a return. Sound travels eight or nine times faster underwater, it's a much better conductor of sound. It is so very simple, yet made sophisticated."

"A U-boat killer?" Luther Rogers said joyously. All the uncertainty of ever sinking a U-boat, or just to see one that had been whittled down to a fragile twig instantly grew once more to redwood proportions. He looked at Petty Officer Jackson as if he were a heavenly warrior with the ferocity of a Viking raider, the strategic wisdom of Alexander the Great, the perseverance of Hannibal, and the graciousness of Suede Bonnet all rolled into five feet ten inches of Coast Guard blue. "I am doubly pleased to have you with us. You probably think you're condemned to nurse a couple of elderly men. But, I can assure you that we are in top shape and ready to go the line. Homer Crown, the other crewmember is the best sailor you'll ever have the pleasure of sailing with. If the wrath of hell opened up on the high seas I would have no other at the sheets."

Max tried to hide his mask of bewilderment. He thought: what are sheets? Are these old farts a couple of fairies? He thought of Luther Rogers and some other wrinkled-up old man sleeping together, between the sheets. No, he embarrassingly realized, he must've been referring to the sails.

Luther Rogers read Max's expression, "Sheets are the lines that control each sail. Like that one," Luther pointed to a rope and traced it out with his finger, "that's the main sheet. It attaches to the horizontal spar called a boom. It's appropriately named because it'll go boom right on the ol' noggin'. The sails trim is primarily controlled by how much sheet you let out. We have two masts, the larger, forward mast is the main and the smaller aft one is the mizzen. There is matching tackle for both, so, the mizzen sheet and the main sheet. I'm boring you, we'll have time to learn."

"Oh, uh-huh. I raced dinghy sailboats with my brother but we never had any formal training." Max smiled, relieved the narrative was over.

Luther faced Petty Officer Jackson and said, "I need your help if I'm going to catch a U-boat."

"No offense, but I doubt we'll ever have to worry about sinking a U-boat. We'd be awfully lucky if we even see one, and then the only thing we could do would be call a destroyer on the wireless. The destroyer is the only thing that can sink a U-boat. A sailboat is too slow, besides, they would see us miles away with these huge sails signaling our position. How far away do you think we're going to be able to see a needle-size periscope?"

With a resounding thud, Luther Rogers' redwood crashed to the earth.

How fast is a U-boat? They probably go thirty knots, he thought. Luther Rogers hated being so ignorant about the enemy's capabilities. The intricacies and perplexities of the deadly creatures he had vowed to kill were so foreign.

Petty Officer Jackson continued, "We have our meeting in two hours. Want to walk over with me?"

Luther studied Maxwell Jackson. The young man could see someone who had sat in the comforts of a plush wood-lined office for over fifty years, wishing to go to war, Luther could see it in his eyes. Nonetheless, those youthful delusions were still alive, to test his character, but not for courage, that vagary had long ago been exhausted, it was preservation that was on the line.

Thirteen

Luther and Max, Captain and XO of *Lady's Revenge, CGR65320* walked side-by-side through the noise and plethora of work being accomplished by the Navy Yard. In a relatively quiet corner of the Yard four brick buildings stood erect, clashing with the charred and rusted motif. They were built just two years prior, the white brick was still holding up against the New York smog. Luther Rogers and Max Jackson entered through glass doors. A hand-written sign was taped to the bulkhead "CORSAIR FLEET " and below it an arrow pointed the direction. Two men walked through the doors, laughed at something, and then said hello as they passed Luther and Max. Following the two men through the door they found two empty foldout chairs halfway down the filled room.

A Navy Captain stood before the group of sailors. A round symbol was taped to the black board. Donald Duck was painted in the center wearing pirate's garb, puffing himself full on the deck of a ship with a dagger in his bill and a pistol in each hand. A boarder around the cartoon spelled, U S COAST GUARD CORSAIR FLEET.

A Coast Guard Admiral walked to the stage to join the Captain. His shoulders were topped with gold boards. His chest revealed past accomplishments: a Navy Cross, Purple Heart, and most of the colors in the spectrum were represented on several ribbons. He cleared his throat. Admiral Kanteel was about to declare the weakness of his service to protect the eastern shipping lanes, to accept defeat, to accept help from civilians.

"Gentlemen, I am delighted to see so many brave men have answered the call. We are in a desperate situation that necessitates the utilization of all our resources. You have volunteered to sail against an enemy who has demonstrated that he will stop at nothing and fight with the most diabolical intensions. They are using the greatest fighting machine created by man. As you know, the U-boat has caused a huge embarrassment to our country. He sails the western Atlantic unmolested, however, that is going to change now...with each and everyone of you." Admiral Kanteel refused to admit that the U-boats were waging a battle of magnitude never experienced by the United States. He continued, "I want each and every one of you to go out there and stop him, the Nazi terrorists. You may never see him, but be sure he, the spineless coward, is hiding under every wave. Your presence out there will ward off the bastards, for he's afraid to fight like a man. He only goes after our helpless merchant mariners.

"Captain Lovejoy will give you assignments and positions. A tactical network of wireless stations has been put into place to keep in constant touch. It is critical to the success of the mission to stay in constant communication, to make your presence known. The more assets and noise we make out there the better we'll be able to scare the bastards off. Anyone who engages in such deceitful warfare is afraid of confrontation with a worthy enemy. Coast Guard cutters will be patrolling in the area, but we are limited in the number of ships that can be used against the Germans. You are our safety net. Let me reemphasize, and you will hear this over and over, do not engage the enemy. I trust you will be vigilant in your duties. Good hunting."

The crowd of anxious Corsair sailors gave a thunderous applause. Captain Lovejoy let the Admiral have his ovation. When the Admiral walked off to a waiting lieutenant aide and disappeared from the room Lovejoy pulled down a chart of the Atlantic. The Captain pointed to various merchant sinking's, the chart was marked with a red dots representing downed freighters. There was no pattern just a free-for-all killing spree for German U-boats on the coastal shipping route.

"The war in the Pacific has left our east virtually unprotected except for a handful of Coast Guard cutters. The safety and survival of our merchant fleet rests upon your brave shoulders. You will receive a confidential list of merchant traffic in your area. You are to screen these ships. Your job will be to deter a U-boat long enough for the merchant vessel to pass safely by unmolested. Most U-boats will avoid detection at all costs. Your small vessels will be a thorn in Hitler's side. God speed."

Luther Rogers was not impressed by the presentation. He did, however, feel apart of a bigger and more complete legion—the sensation of being closer to that test of manhood he had so long desired, like the feeling of being closer to God in a cathedral, he felt that same sensation in this war room. Luther shared the Captain's sentiment that the Germans were heinous villains, killing young, defenseless merchant mariners. He did not fear the Nazis. Visions of soldiers unloading at the train station came back to mind. Luther remembered a young man, eighteen at the most, who smiled at the sight of New York as he hopped off the Pennsylvania car, his leg missing from the hip. His face, suffering from acne and a long scar that ran from his ear to his smile, glowed. Luther watched as the young soldier breathed in New York and was happy and grateful to be home.

Luther stood outside and breathed in New York, happy and grateful for this opportunity, for this war. Max looked at the old man. "You okay mister?"

Luther didn't turn but answered, "I'm taking it all in."

"Suit yourself old man," Max said under his breath as he left the man inhaling the pollution of the Navy Yard. Why couldn't I be in the Pacific? The war was officially passing him by.

Fourteen

Max gazed out the huge window at the Point Lookout Marina. Luther Rogers came up behind the Sonarman. "Great view isn't it?"

"Yes," Max nodded. "This window is gigantic." Max eyed the dimensions.

"You two tourists want to get back to work?" Homer called out. He sat in a metal folding chair behind a card table littered with charts and papers.

Max and Luther returned to take their positions at the table. They had been discussing plans for their patrol all morning, and Luther was tired. He rubbed the fatigue out of his eyes. Homer continued like a stodgy old school master. "I like your plan for doing this search pattern," he looked up at Max Jackson. "It would give symmetry to our patrolling area. With this merchant fleet traffic list I want to see that none are torpedoed in our sector. If we position ourselves just so," he pointed, "we could launch our depth charges. Sink the Nazi scum!"

"Excuse me, Mister Rogers, would you be needing anything else? I've got to get down to Hanson's boat. Wants me to scrub 'er down," Rich Blazak said after setting up the coffee urn. He stood overlooking the charts with idle curiosity. His appearance resembled a man who fell into a Salvation Army donation bin naked and crawled out—wellington boots, paint-stained trousers, a wool red and black hunting jacket topped off with a green Sou'wester. Rich Blazak walked with a limp, not from any leg injuries, but instead exposure from mustard gas dropped into the trench he was guarding in Belgium.

"No thank you, Richard. I appreciate everything." Luther liked the dockhand.

"I think when you get out there you'll discover that it doesn't matter where we patrol, or how. We aren't going to see any U-boats. We're just some political ploy." Max was becoming irritated with the over-planning. He felt like he was going over this dumb patrol like it was some split-second, precise strategy to win the war.

Homer Crown was a scary zealot. Even to Max, Homer's lust for German blood was disconcerting, the nonstop reference to killing Nazis had become intolerable. Max had no opportunity to really know the man, save for his bloodlust.

"Forgive me. If you don't want to be here to discuss important issues such as strategy then take your little yellow ass and get the hell out of here."

"That's uncalled for Homer. Please, no hostilities. We're all getting tired." Luther Rogers glared accusingly at Homer Crown. Homer got the message.

Max attempted to sooth the tone. "I understand the strategy and I know how to sink a U-boat with the depth charges. I just need a break. We've been going at it all day. Until we get the boat back and can start training all this is for not." Max was exhausted, but he decided to placate the old man. "Mister Crown, how come you're braving such a patrol with the picket duty?"

Homer didn't like the condescending sound of the question. "I have my reasons you little urchin."

Max persisted, undaunted by Homer's contemptuousness, "Really, why? If we're going to serve together I should know. You don't have to do this, I do."

There was certain logic to Max's reasoning that not even the despiteful Homer Crown could deny. "Maybe you're right," Homer conceded. Homer stood and walked to the window. He stared out silently and then thought better of it. He felt the energy drain, stepped back to the fold out chair and sat. He blankly looked at the chart and said, "I lost my family."

"Oh. . .I'm sorry." Max didn't pry to get the details. He really didn't know what to say or how to feel, like being at a funeral, attempting condolences to the bereaved.

"Why should you be sorry?" Homer Crown was seventy-four-years-old, old enough to understand the awkwardness Max was experiencing.

"Homer, please. The kid is trying to be nice." Luther said.

"Kid, you'll be alright. Just stop acting like some damn diaper boy."

Luther Rogers stood up and began collecting the charts scattered on the table. "We should all go home."

Max agreed.

Max sat in the passenger's seat as Luther Rogers drove the Lincoln back to Brooklyn. "Why are you doing this, Mister Rogers?"

Luther Rogers shifted gears. He didn't look at Max but gazed forward. "Want to stop by Garzezo's for some late dinner and a drink?"

"Sure, that would be nice."

Garzezo's was a run down diner in Bethpage. Garzezo had inherited the small restaurant from his uncle and had done nothing in the way of improving the décor, which was exactly its appeal. Luther slid into one of the four booths, the red leather upholstery was stained brown and cracked, gas lamps recently converted to accept electric bulbs hung from the wall. Harriet came over, her hair in a bonnet neat and tidy even after twelve hours on the floor.

"Hi, Harriet. I'll take a grilled cheese and a beer." One of the many uniqueness's of Garzezo's was they served homemade beer and had done so for fifty years with no break for prohibition.

"Could I see a menu?"

"There ain't none, sugar. You tell me what you want and I'll get it for you."

"A grilled turkey and swiss and a beer." Max ordered, half-expecting her to refuse the order. She walked away as if she had been doing it all her life, which in fact she had.

The dinner plates came and Max was surprised with the size of the bread, it almost filled the entire plate.

Luther Rogers took a long draw from his draught. "This is why I come to this place, the best beer you're to find in all of New York."

Max drank his beer, he didn't share Luther's taste for the local brew and it didn't mix well with the turkey and Swiss.

"What do you think will happen if Hitler takes over the U. S.?" Max asked.

"I never thought about it. That's a pretty scary thought. I'm too old to care I suppose. Japan and Germany would probably fight over us."

"This war isn't going very good for us."

Luther knew the United States was losing the war. "I think you'll see that no one can beat us. Just like now, we're rallying together to fight off German U-boats."

"That's it exactly, we're so desperate the country's turning to old men and sailboats to fight one of the most advanced weapons produced by man. Doesn't that tell you how pathetic our situation is? The more I think of it the more it scares me."

Luther Rogers had never rationalized the situation quite that way, that the United States was doomed and the Corsair fleet was one of the last-ditch efforts. "Believe it or not the automobile industry is going to save us," he predicted, with a weak attempt of optimism, for the whole, crazy world-gone-mad war.

Max looked at him sideways, "Huh?"

"Max, the United States has the largest automobile industry in the world. We'll stop making automobiles and start making tanks, and planes, and artillery. We are going to out-produce the world in weapons necessary for war." Luther sipped his beer and then continued, "The enemy is too far away to mount a real invasion force, and even if they did they couldn't keep it supplied. We might lose Europe and Asia, but America will survive."

"I sure hope you're right. I never thought about that before. I just wish I could be over there with real fighting men. I'm sorry, but it's how I feel," Max added flush with guilt for blurting out the insult.

"I understand. We're a couple of old farts holding you back. But trust me when I say that we owe you our lives in that you have given us something to live for. We will not disappoint you with enthusiasm and dedication." Luther dropped five dollars on the table, "Well, are you ready to get out of here?"

Max didn't care how much dedication and enthusiasm they offered him, it was still babysitting and he hated it.

Fifteen

Leighton Avenue ran the length of Yonkers north and south, but it was at the north end, farthest from the city where the mansions of new wealth lined the avenue. Brass streetlamps dotted the lane. The Coopersmith's occupied a three-story Victorian that jumped out of the pages of a Henry James novel. The manicured front lawn was small in comparison, but it made up for what it lacked with a porch that could seat a church parish. The back yard was large enough to have a tournament-sized croquet court, a tennis court, and a 1/2-acre flower garden. Maples stood, towering over the property they surrounded, as a natural barricade.

Harry Coopersmith sat in his kitchen, drinking coffee, watching his wife fry eggs. She had denied her husband a paid cook, insisting on doing the chore herself. He felt his swelled stomach. Harry was fortunate to have kept his waist all through the years as his friends' inched bigger and bigger. He thought it strange to be so full and still be starving for three over-easy.

"How have you managed to keep your figure all these years?" Harry said, admiring his wife's backside.

Patty Coopersmith blushed. Harry knew nothing of chromosomes, but nonetheless still admired the genes that kept his wife vibrant and sexy. The years had not diminished her appeal. Patty, lucky with the distribution of those few extra pounds that twenty years of marriage brought, still commanded admiring looks from passing males. She swirled around and eyed her husband, "I'm so busy cooking for you I haven't got time to eat."

"Do you still love me? Even if I only love you for your cooking?"

"Harry, shut-up and eat. Of course I love you. What's wrong with you? You've been acting strange the last couple of days."

"I don't know. I guess I've been thinking about those old men I helped get on picket duty. They seem so focused on saving the country, it seems so noble."

"You are doing noble things, too. You're helping people escape from all this terrible business. People need a way to vent all that anxiety, and you've given it to them." Mrs. Coopersmith supported her husband faithfully, blindly. She did not agree with his profession, operating three racetracks and a trucking business that catered to the mob, but it was her husband's ambition and therefore hers.

"I guess you're right. I . . ." Harry was interrupted by the door chimes. "I wonder who that could be this early in the day?"

"It's probably Mrs. Cairns," Patty said, wiping her hands on a bright green dishtowel.

"Tell her we'll be done making' whoopee in a second, unless of course she'd like to watch, the nosey little nuisance."

"Oh, Harry. Be nice."

Patty opened the giant, ornate mahogany door. Instead of finding her next-door neighbor she saw a boy dressed in a yellow uniform with bow tie.

"Harold Coopersmith?"

"I'm Misses Coopersmith."

"Sorry ma'am, I have a telegram."

"I'll take it."

Patty signed the boy's pad and took the telegram. She turned it over, and held it up to the morning sunlight, attempting to see the contents. Walking slowly across the Persian rug, she examined it in a way that suggested her vision was x-ray.

Handing it to her husband upon returning to the kitchen, she hovered over him impatiently. She was anxious with curiosity to find out what was written on the telegram, she'd never seen one before.

Harry received them daily at the office from breeders and racetracks, he set it to the side.

"Well, aren't you even going to open it?"

"I was going to finish eating."

Patty sat down and stared at him while he lifted a fork full of eggs.

"Alright, let's see what's inside. I bet it's those old farts sending a thank you."

Harry opened the envelope and pulled out the yellow paper. Patty stretched to look, she was surprised to see stop at the end of each sentence.

He read.

"What's it say?"

Sixteen

In the autumn of '41 on the campus of Princeton, like college campuses all over the world, war floated in and out of every conversation. The havens of intellectual discourse were saturated with the proposition and topic of war. In the United States it was stay out, get in on the action, stop aggression, suppression, where's the justification, intolerance for belligerence, fascism: the political ruse—nowhere in the university environment was intercourse safe from war. The Japanese had yet to bomb Pearl Harbor when the younger Coopersmith was engaged in the heated debates. Europe and China however were very much at war.

Michael Coopersmith took the usual liberal arts classes his freshman year, along with chemistry 101. It was in chemistry lab that he became friends with

Kim Lee, a Chinese-American student from Portland, Oregon. He had never known a Chinese-American, sure he had seen them in Chinatown, but they might as well have been Martians. He could overhear her laugh and recap the usual college freshman stories about her antics over the weekends. She was exotic. She was erotic. She was foreign and young and Coopersmith could not help but feel the sexual lure of this oriental creature. The straight black hair that shown as if it were waxed to high gloss, the petite frame and small breasts that were just detectable under the white lab coat—he was smitten. Soon he managed to get a date that was followed by several, until it finally arrived at a point where they enjoyed routine morning strolls through campus followed by an evening at the campus hang-out Carlisle's for coffee or beer. During their hours learning about each other Michael began listening. He eased into the weight of Kim Lee's narratives slowly, like easing into a hot bath. But soon, the plight of the Chinese against the Japanese aggression in Kim Lee's homeland found Michael's heart and buried its hook deep into his consciousness. He had, despite all his contrary beliefs regarding racism, by his junior year become a flagrant bigot. He participated in the debates about the war in China with over-enthusiastic ferocity—he hated the Japanese. His classmates began to expect such vindictiveness that they avoided such hostile topics in his presence.

It was because of Michael's growing passion and anti-Japanese views that he would sit in his dorm room scheming. He was resolute to do something about the Japanese Asian conquest. Michael Coopersmith, armed with youthful delusions and confidence, was going to crush the rising sun in the Pacific. The vindictiveness turned an entire race into a sub-human, evil form that manifested itself in Michael's rants. The hatred burned in him.

His roommate, Nick Moffett, loathed time alone with his dorm mate. He often tried to hide the newspaper so that a war story would not trigger Michael into some psychotic rage about the evil yellow monsters from Japan. Moffett leaned against a stack of pillows on his bed reading The Collected Letters of Robinson Jeffers when it hit him. He snapped his fingers and then wrote a message to Mike to meet him at Carlisle's.

Later that night, Nick sat back in a booth with a freshly poured lager in front of him on the old dark table. Finally, Michael slid in across from Nick. It was obvious that Nick had been there for a while from the slur in his greeting.

"Why the meeting roomie?"

Nick took another swig of beer and then began, "Mike, my dear boy, you should write a series of letters to home." Nick slurred something, took another pull on the lager. "See this is how'd it work. . .."

"You called me here to tell me to write letters home? As if I don't already."

"Exactly!" Nick said. "I could deposit your letters perry-ode-ick," Nick swallowed hard and continued, "periodically deposit them at the Post Office. Throughout the year, roomie. To home."

"Why would I want you to do that?" Michael became irritated.

"You need a beer, Mike. Oh, barman, could you pour a beer for my friend." Nick pointed a finger at Michael, almost poking his eye. "Mike, my roomie, your parent's wouldn't know for least a semester." Nick snickered then accelerated into full-blown laughter. The laughter was contagious, even though Mike had no idea what he was giggling about.

Nick continued, ". . . send them a Christmas card announcing your acceptance of an invitation to holiday at the Moffett's. All the while, you're off to become a Marine."

"A WHAT?"

"A Marine. You could go kill them Japs you're always talking about."

Michael sat silently as the bartender unceremoniously slammed a mug of beer in front of him. He took a swallow, wiped the foam from his lips with the back of his hand, and then looked into the glassy brown eyes of his drunk friend. A Marine. He'd have to do some research about the Marine Corps. But it was a grand idea! "I'll do it," Michael whispered.

"I'll do it," Michael said loud enough for his drunken roommate to hear.

Nick dropped his beer to the table, "What? Are you mad?"

"It was you're idea."

"I know it was my idea, but that was five beers back and now I don't know what the hell I'm saying. Join the blasted Marine Corps, kills Japs, you're insane."

"Jeez, Nick you brought it up."

"Yeah, but I brought up having a go at Mrs. Clarke in English lit too. Don't mean it's a good idea. She's probably forty-five at least. Great boobs though, huh?"

"Stay focused, Nick. We're talking about me joining the Marine Corps. I could finally do something meaningful with my life instead of listening to professors drone away about ancient bullshit." The more he thought about it the more Michael liked the idea. His thoughts raced at break-neck speed. "I'm going to do it. Where is there a Marine Corps recruiter? Let's go see him right now. You could come with me."

Nick tried to focus on his roommate. "Are you crazy! I have to send your damned letters to mommy. I don't want to kill Japs, they haven't done nothing to me." Oh shit, Nick thought, he just opened the can of worms. He cringed waiting for the verbal onslaught, but it didn't come. Michael Coopersmith was already in a Marine Corps uniform killing Japanese, Nick could see it in his eyes, although somewhat blurry in focus.

Three weeks later Nick Moffett accompanied his roommate to the train station. The occasion was somber as the two young men shook hands and held back any real emotion. Michael Coopersmith found his seat and settled in for the long, nervous ride to Parris Island, the Marine Corps training facility. He waved out the train car window as his roommate disappeared from view as the train proceeded out of the station.

Seventeen

Private Coopersmith survived the rigorous demands of learning to become a U.S. Marine. He learned how to clean his Springfield .03, clean his squad bay, clean and polish his boots, clean and press his wool uniform, clean the head, clean the galley, clean the dirt, to clean just about everything except for his vocabulary. Michael Coopersmith learned how to swear like a Marine. It was a language not colloquial at Princeton, but it certainly was fitting at Parris Island. He was thoroughly disappointed in his training to kill Japs, but usually he was too tired to put much thought to it. After graduation he turned down leave so it was off to San Diego to board a transport ship loaded with equipment and men that sailed for Pearl Harbor. They arrived in the tropical paradise after an eight-day transit. Private Coopersmith viewed the U.S. Navy battlewagons in the harbor from the deck of the transport, he knew they were named after states but he couldn't find his home state, New York, if there even was a ship named after the empire state. After a week in Hawaii, unloading and repacking and no liberty, the transport ship cast off lines and headed to sea, destination: Wake Atoll.

Private Coopersmith saw why he had never heard mention of Wake Island, it was a barren outcropping of sand-covered coral. He was disappointed; no palm trees grew, no port nor harbor, nothing save for a few wind-blown shrubs and tin buildings. This was where he was going to destroy Japanese belligerence?

"Welcome home," a young Marine said, his hair too short to discern any color. "Get off my fuckin' beach and find a fuckin' tent," the sergeant barked. "Shit, nice to meet you too," Patty replied. Patty was the only Marine in Mike's boot camp platoon to make the Pacific journey with him. Mike always thought of his mother whenever anyone would call the young private. His real name was William Patriolli from Youngstown, Ohio, the third son of a second-generation steel worker but to everyone he was known simply as Patty.

A seasoned Marine came at them. "Go dig a fuckin' hole and crawl in it, boot. You want me to kick your ass all the way to your rack like a tin can?"

Private Coopersmith took hold of Patty's rucksack strap and pulled him toward the row of tents. "Come on Patty, don't piss 'em off on the first day."

Patty looked at his comrade and stopped as he viewed the island. "Holy shit, they've got to be kidding. There's nothing here."

"This is the Corps, boot. Semper Fi," the sergeant said as he passed by.

Mike's heart sank. This was not how he imagined his dream; stranded on a hunk of sand in the middle of the Pacific. He was certain the Japanese would not waste their time with such a far-removed void in the middle of nowhere. The Marine Corps must've had a sense of humor to pick this worthless piece of real estate to set up an airfield. A large wave could simply roll right over the entire island.

Walking toward the messdeck tent, Private Coopersmith was greeted by a large reception of fellow Marines and civilians cheering with disorganized rants and hoo-hahs. He was impressed at their enthusiastic welcome for a handful of new arrivals, but it wasn't him they were welcoming, it was the mail.

On the tenth day, December fifth, Mike realized that he had traded interesting lectures in philosophy, discussions of insight and a comfortable dorm room for slave labor and half a tent. He dug trenches in the morning, erected frames for makeshift buildings in the afternoon, and set up battery positions in the evening. Every fucking day.

Still no Japanese to kill. Private Coopersmith was more convinced that he would never see a Jap. But, the United States was still not in the war.

"Do you want those?"

Mike looked at Patty spying his hard roll, the bread made on the island seemed to redefine the laws of density for wheat— granite would float better than the Marine-made bread. "It's really not that bad for island food. I couldn't imagine how much it costs to supply this asshole of the world," Patty said.

Mike tossed the roll to Patty, "They send us this shit, just like a real asshole. And, we're shit for being here." Mike thought about the logistics of supplying so many men, and there was not a single woman on the island. "Toilet paper."

"Huh." Patty looked at him, his jaw steadily working on a piece of hard bread.

"Who has to buy the toilet paper? And, the toothpaste, and all the other little things?"

"The only thing made here is sandbags. Fucking Sand. Fucking Bags. Sand goes into the cute little bags. I'll leave the Corps with a skill. A skill to fill these gorgeous burlap bags right out of the pages of Better Fucking Homes and Garden."

Mike was embarrassed by the accusation, no matter how true it was. "I would give anything to be back in the States. I didn't join to fill bags with sand. The food is rotten. Everything is god-awful horrible, like I've committed myself to Devil's Island."

"I want to make a little whoopee. No, I want to make a lot of whoopee! These ten days have seemed like ten years." Patty laughed caught up in Coopersmith's laments, and then Mike joined in. "You know, if we keep this up we're going to bag the entire island and then where will we be?" They both erupted in a guffaw that caught the other Marines attention.

A leathery old man, Mike saw how Marines got their nickname leathernecks, entered the mess deck. "Okay, boots let's get back to work."

On the eighth of December a report was issued over the radio that Pearl Harbor was under attack, Wake Atoll was across the International dateline, and therefore one day ahead. Major Devereux, the Marine commander, ordered everyone to battle stations. Mike took his position in a trench circling Battery A at the spear tip shaped end of the island. Private Mike Coopersmith gazed out at the sea breaking on the outlying reef. The noise from the surf was continuous, monotonous. He wished he had been left at Pearl Harbor to fight the damn Japs. Instead, he was abandoned out on this miserable chunk of coral, forgotten by the Americans, but more disconcerting, forgotten by the damned Japanese. He imagined himself fighting the Japanese landing on the shores of Hawaii. He would kill them all; first with his Springfield, then with his bayonet. He would take them all out, save the platoon, save the world.

His father would never understand. His father, Mister Harold Coopersmith, was too concerned with his image, status in New York men's clubs, and most of all, with money. Mike could not envision his father being concerned with any political view if it did not make a profit. His father was selfish and clueless about what it meant to have a meaningful cause. A reason for living. Mike looked around at his home now, what a fucking miserable hellhole, forgotten on this piss-ant sand knoll.

The day passed uneventfully. The Japs would skip right over this anal orifice of the world.

"We got lucky."

Mike thrust his fist into a sandbag. "How so, Patty?"

Patty looked at his friend as if he were a total stranger. "What do ya mean, how so? The Japanese are attacking Pearl Harbor, not us. I don't want to fight no damn slant eyes. I heard they eat their prisoners."

Mike didn't appreciate slant eyes. "Call 'em yellow monkeys, nips, japs, but not slant eyes that's too vague. I joined to fight."

"Mister Marine Corps. We all joined to fight, but look around you. We would be outnumbered, trying to defend a sand dune with only sea oats to hide behind. No thanks, I ain't stupid."

The next morning, Mike woke to the sound of rain splattering on his tent. He joined Patty in the trench on the beachhead. They had to yell above the sound of the rain and surf. The sensation of being forgotten was worse. He put his round doughboy style helmet on his head and amused himself with watching the rain cascade over the sides like little miniature waterfalls. It was almost noon he guessed, almost time for lunch—meals were one of the only pleasures to break the daily grind.

At least they weren't filling sand bags and working on the damned runway.

Suddenly, three 12-plane vees swooped down out of the clouds. Their roaring engines audible above the surf and rain. Mike stood up, gazing motionless at the incoming planes. He forgot all of his training.

The first bomb exploded, waking Mike from his trance. Eight wildcats were being fueled on the runway. Mike turned to watch, he cringed as four of the fighters exploded into nothingness. Three of the other planes caught fire and soon were reduced to skeletons. Calmly, Mike raised his rifle at one of the Jap bombers swooping down toward him and fired. He smelled the smoke, he felt the recoil, a culmination of all his aggression flowed through his limbs and out the barrel. He was numb with outrage, Mike slammed the bolt home repeatedly, round after round. He kept pulling the trigger and bolting home each round, until the rifle was empty.

"Coopersmith, get the hell down here!" Patty pulled Mike back down into the protection of the sandbags.

"Did you see that? Those were yellow-monkey Japs. Japanese planes. They didn't forget us after all!"

Patty gave his friend a queer look. "Shit, look at this mess. You're nuts."

"Patriolli, Sullivan, Hertzog and Coopersmith, get topside to help with clean-ups," Lieutenant Barninger said as he walked pass.

The sight of the dead bodies drowned the excitement of the attack. Mike gazed at the civilians and Marines that were scattered across the runway like discarded rag dolls. They collected the dead men onto burlap stretchers and laid them into neat rows. A backhoe was digging their grave. What was left of the planes was being bulldozed off into heaps surrounding the runway. All the while it rained. Mike worked around the clock, with only occasional breaks for a nap, to rebuild the damaged buildings and airfield.

Eighteen

The tenth of December the rain stopped the bombing started. Mike, trudging through the sand back from a work party, dove into a nearby trench. A great thunder shook the earth as 125 tons of dynamite went up and the air filled suddenly with dust and debris. The rain was gone now to keep it down. Mike found it hard to breath, the smell of death, the cloud of dust, and burning smell of sulfur suffocated him. He buried his face into the sand as pellets of coral dropped on his back. It seemed like hours, but finally the bombers exhausted all their armament and left the island in chaos. Men screamed and barked out commands while others cried out for help. Mike belly-crawled back to his position at Battery A, relieved to be home in his sandbag trench.

Patty was anxiously waiting for him. "My God, are you all right? This shit's for the fucking birds!"

Mike thought for the birds was grossly inadequate. How did he talk himself into thinking he was going to crush the Japanese empire? He wanted nothing more than to be safe and sound in his father's house. He crouched down in the trench, fear pumped through him like a caustic acid.

Patty examined Mike. "The Navy will send a task force soon enough. They don't want to lose this invaluable airstrip."

"Invaluable! Look around at the damn thing." The runway, which had been fresh with newly poured concrete was broken and scattered. Planes that had lined the tarmac were strewn pieces of steel and aluminum and rubber. The airstrip was unrecognizable. "We're just sitting ducks, target practice for the Japanese air force." Mike retorted. He was struggling to keep back the tears.

The morning of December Eleventh, Mike was paralyzed at the sight of Japanese ships offshore. He shivered at the thought of applying those silly lessons in hand-to-hand combat. He felt the weight of his Springfield rifle and his bayonet, he suddenly felt very inadequate to fight Japanese.

Kabang! A tremendous report sang out, deafening the young Marines in the trench. The salvo was from the five-inch battery guns manned by Marines with Pan-Am civilians hauling ammunition as it barked out a challenge to the Japanese aggressors. Mike held his ears tight with his palms and cringed with each shot. Water plums formed around the Jap destroyer. One, two, and then three or was it four? Four rounds found home. The destroyer was alive with fire and smoke. She turned and disappeared momentarily in a smoke screen. She ran for the horizon.

"Yes! Yee ha." Patty was jumping up and down. A cheer sounded from their end of the island as the burning destroyer retreated.

"Look." Mike pointed toward the west side of the island. A destroyer was exploding and sinking all in the same defiant motion. They had defeated the Japanese. Mike's courage rebounded.

The Japanese had to soften up the foe so they resorted back to air tactics. Bombing and strafing runs continued daily. Mike was exhausted. He was not alone. He wanted to collapse and dream away this ridiculous thing called war. The rumor that no help was to come alternated with the rumor that *Saratoga*'s task force was just out of reach. He was sick of it. No more. But the Japanese continued their unrelenting bombing and soon there was nothing left recognizable of the airstrip.

Christmas was only two days away. As Mike lay half-buried in sand, he wondered if it was snowing in New York. He thought of storefronts and wreaths that would line the streets of Manhattan. New York, would they know what was happening here on this little speck in the Pacific?

He was exhausted but didn't dare sleep.

Patty crawled over to his friend's section of the trench. "Mike, we've got to go with Captain Alright to reinforce a Battery position." As he said the new orders a fresh wave of gunfire could be heard lighting up the sky.

"No. I don't want to go." Mike horrified a Japanese landing might occur.

"You have to. Get up."

"Why? I can stay here, it's not going to make any difference. The island's too small to worry about positions."

Finally, Mike reluctantly got up from his sand hole and followed Patty.

Mike and Patty joined the civilian contractors and flight crews from the ill-fated VMF-211. The guns hammered into the night at unseen forces. A boat on the beach exploded and for the first time Mike saw the Japanese Marines, or the Rikusentai. About a thousand black silhouettes covered the beach, inching their way forward. Someone yelled out to fix bayonets. Mike instinctively followed the order. The civilians were the first to open fire. Soon the entire row of men lit up with bore bursts. A man ran behind the line giving each a handful of grenades.

Patty tapped Mike on the shoulder. He was irritated that someone would break his concentration, but relieved just the same. Patty smiled at him, Mike couldn't help but to smile back. There was a yell in the darkness and off to Mike's left Japs started swarming into the shallow trench. To his right a shadow appeared. It was coming at him. Mike raised his rifle and fired. There was a scream but the shadow kept coming. Patty yelled with rage but stopped suddenly as if the wind were punched out of him, a Japanese bullet had found him. Blood streamed, staining Patty's chest. Patty's gaze rose to meet one of the shadows that materialized into a Japanese Marine. The Jap ran his long bayonet through the center of Patty. Patty griped the rifle and wouldn't let the Rikusentai retrieve his weapon. Mike swung his rifle and fired, causing the Jap's face to explode into a mist of flesh and bone. Mike bolted another round into the chamber of his Springfield, found a target and fired. He did not waste a single round, each bullet found a Jap.

There were too many. He could no longer take the time to reload so he jumped out of the trench and rammed his stock into the face of a charging Japanese Rikusentai. The Jap's nose shattered, he crouched down holding his face. The next man he stabbed with his bayonet. He withdrew the blade and found another Jap to stick. Mike lunged forward. His bayonet ran into the chest of yet another Jap. He tried to extract the rifle-mounted knife but it was wedged in between the ribs and wouldn't budge.

Mike looked up in terror. He struggled with the dead man to no avail. A Rikusentai lanced him in the shoulder. Mike fell back. The Jap glanced into Mike's eyes, yanked the bayonet out and ran off. Mike, sprawled out on the sand, watched the Rikusentai run by. One stopped and looked down at him. Mike raised his hands for help and surrender but the man stared back and plunged a bayonet into Mike's abdomen. Mike gripped the hole that the fleeing man left. He gagged. This was not how it was supposed to be. Another Japanese, feeling left out, jabbed his bayonet through Mike's left thigh, pulling sand back up through the wound. Mike screamed at the pain. The Jap smiled and fled with the rest.

Now Mike was alone. He couldn't move. He gazed at the stars above and thought how brilliant they were. He slipped into thoughts of New York and his father's house. Would his father get his letters? Michael Coopersmith never saw the sun rise.

Nineteen

Harry Coopersmith was void of all thoughts. He stared at the half-eaten breakfast on his plate. The telegram fell from his fingers and floated to the tile floor. Sitting hunched over in the kitchen chair he looked at the yolk drain from one of the eggs.

Patty retrieved the telegram. She read it and whaled as her whole body trembled.

Harry talked to no one except himself, "I thought he was at Princeton. He didn't tell me. It's a mistake. He's at Princeton. He can't be in the Marine Corps. He's at Princeton. MICHAEL'S AT PRINCETON!"

Twenty

A light snow covered the outer barrier island on Long Island's south shore, Long Beach located on a thin strip of land that formed a break wall from the Atlantic. Large summer homes rose from the sand like a long palisade. This was the original summer getaway, closer to the city than the Hamptons. The sky was split, night on one side, day on the other. Five-thirty, the sun would not rise into view for another hour. Harry Coopersmith followed the footsteps in the snow, stopping at the dock edge.

"Hello! Anybody there?"

A noise was audible from down below. Harry stepped over the reach of water onto the deck of the gray boat. He barely recognized the Hinckley as the one he had seen earlier. Somehow though, despite the gray institutionalization of it, the yacht still held its majesty. The boat rolled slightly from the foreign weight. He set his bag down as the hatch clicked then slid open, revealing Homer Crown.

"Coopersmith? What are you doing here?"

"Good morning, Mister Crown. Is Luther Rogers aboard?"

"Yes." Homer made no attempt to announce the guest.

"May I speak with him?"

Homer grunted and vanished in the shadow below. Harry heard a muffled discussion, and then Luther Rogers appeared followed by Homer Crown.

"Good morning, Mister Coopersmith. It's so kind of you to come down and see us off." Luther Rogers could not help but be thankful for the impossible Harry had achieved.

"Good morning to you also. I want to go with you." The news of Harry's son's death on some insignificant island had left the father incapable of formalities that he once considered an art. "I will not be refused."

"Harry, what has brought this about? Why the sudden interest to go out with some old crazy men with one foot in the grave?"

"Michael." It was obvious Luther Rogers didn't understand. Harry continued, "You need an extra hand. I know how to sail, I'm good. I brought extra stores." Harry pointed to Rich Blazak approaching, his arms loaded with boxes. Harry looked him square, "You owe me."

"I don't understand?" Luther knew what Harry said was true. Four hands aboard would ease the patrol. He couldn't argue. However, Homer Crown could.

"Harry, you're not our type. This could be a long patrol. It would be miserable with us feuding."

"You're right Homer. It's probably going to be long, boring, and miserable enough without some unwelcome newcomer. But, I need this. Think above yourself, think of the greater cause. I want to kill the damn heartless murders who killed my son."

Harry Coopersmith delivered the only argument that could persuade Homer Crown. Had he used any patriotic hype, political rhetoric, or any other thousand reasons it would not have been convincing; but, to rape that which raped, to kill that which killed, to take revenge, that was a logic that Homer Crown knew, tasted, embraced. Homer Crown swallowed his previous opinion of Harry. He saw something in his eye that he'd never seen before. Truth.

"I won't argue with you, Harry."

The two men shook hands, a cautious agreement. Luther Rogers was eager to have another crewmember. The tree was starting to grow again.

"Is this our entire crew? Three men?" Harry asked skeptically.

Luther Rogers was waiting to announce his ace-in-the-hole, of all the weapons aboard he was proudest of Petty Officer Jackson. "No, we have a highly trained U-boat killer."

"When does he get here? I thought we were supposed to leave at six this morning?"

Homer offered a little smirk. Luther Rogers said, "He's below sleeping."

"Sleeping off a terrible hang-over," Homer said, chuckling.

"Let's get your things below." Luther Rogers wanted to change the subject. He could not tolerate his warrior to be tarnished. He thought back to the many faces he saw coming and going in Union Station. Jackson reminded Luther of the young soldiers he watched from his glass office, the one's that exited the Pullman cars with great difficulty. Luther could only imagine what atrocity the poor bastards had suffered to gain the expressions they wore, or the lost limbs that crippled them. He didn't know why he thought of that scene now. Jackson was an able-bodied young man and not an unknown one-legged private from fifty years ago.

With Harry now a member of the crew of *Lady's Revenge*, or more appropriately now *CGR65320*, they took in the mooring lines as she set out on her first patrol. Orders had come down to patrol the shipping lanes just south of the entrance to New York Harbor. Luther steered the yacht south, through the barrier island entrance. Luther nodded for Homer to take the helm and he rechecked for the umpteenth time the patrol box he drew on the chart off New Jersey coast not far from where he saw the *R. P. Resor* go down back in February. It still amazed him the speed in which everything had happened, thanks to Harry Coopersmith and the United States Coast Guard.

The starboard fore-halyard winch clicked as the main sheet was hauled in. The sun was just over the horizon. Light glowed from the brass compass housing. Unseen from the cockpit the sound of water lapping against the bow filled the dawn. *Lady's Revenge* was underway.

Homer Crown flipped his collar up and tightened his scarf.

Harry surfaced with a steaming pot of coffee. "Would anyone like some java? Captain?"

"Thanks," Luther said holding out his stained ceramic mug.

"Thanks, Harry," Homer whispered, cupping the mug with both hands. He twisted his hip to move the large holstered revolver strapped to his side.

The lights from Long Beach were gone now. The sails were full, the sixty-five foot Hinckley heeled as the sound of water being broken by the bow indicated an increase in speed.

"Let's change to a genoa!" Luther ordered. He pulled in the mizzen sheet. Harry Coopersmith and Homer Crown walked forward like trained hands.

Together, as if they had worked side-by-side for years, they pulled out the 130% genoa. Homer attached the lead to the halyard and shroud while Harry took a turn on the capstan set in the deck port side of the mainmast. Harry hauled in the cotton halyard as Homer guided the new sail on to the runner eyes. The white sail stretched taut. Harry made fast the genoa halyard, and then with skill let the jib halyard run through the capstan, lowering the smaller foresail. Harry Coopersmith admitted to himself that Homer Crown was still a young man.

The sun popped up from its hiding place beneath a ring of clouds that hovered above the horizon off in the distance. The warmth from its radiance was immediate. Luther smiled with thoughts that *Lady's Revenge* had not lost a single knot of speed with the new paint. He poked his head through the lifelines to survey the ocean rushing by. The new sails creaked and stretched. She felt fast. The log indicated thirteen knots.

Homer and Harry returned to the cockpit, chuckling about something funny. Luther had feared the two might be disastrous to the harmony of his small crew, he was glad to see that his initial precaution was invalid.

"Exactly how does this thing work, what are we supposed to do out here? Chasing U-boats and all?" Harry Coopersmith asked, looking at Homer. Homer looked toward Luther. Luther eyed the hatch to the cabin.

"I'm glad you brought that up. Everything has happened so fast that I'm afraid I've neglected the most important aspect of our mission, spent all my time just getting *Lady* ready to sail. Of course, I think the Navy neglected us also. We're now a vessel of the United States Coast Guard, therefore a certain degree of discipline should be maintained. If not for the Coast Guard, then for Petty Officer Jackson. I don't want him to regret sailing with a bunch of old bozzos instead of fighting Japs in the Pacific. Officially,

I'm in command. Petty Officer Jackson is second-in-command, then Homer, and then you, Harry."

"If it gets down to me, I'll be sure to order myself around hast with."

"Geez, it's been too damned long since I've been out here. Colder than I remember," Homer said slapping his arms.

Luther looked at the deck gun and then the racks on the back filled with barrels. "I'm shocked at the training we received."

"I guess I missed out on the important details," Harry said.

Luther smiled at Harry, "we didn't get any either. They painted our boat, mounted the machine gun and depth charges, an underwater microphone— Jackson calls it something fancy—and shoved us off. Good hunting."

"That's it?" Harry was astonished.

Homer slapped his sidearm. "I guess I'll be prepared. When the Coastie gets up we better have him train us how to use these weapons, immediately." Homer was delighted to see the machine gun standing like a sentry. It dominated the foc's'l, the oversized barrel, a sleeve that contained water to cool the inner barrel, was a formidable presence. The depth charge launcher, however, was indiscernible. It was nothing more than a steel frame to hold what looked like oil drums. The depth charges themselves possessed no visual intimidating significance; nonetheless, those drums were filled with incredible explosives that could crush the hull of a U-boat and all the men inside. The high-pressure air activated an arm that pushed the depth charges up and away from *Lady's Revenge*. That innocent steel rack on the stern was the only true weapon against their enemy.

At noon the temperature was just above freezing. The sun was bright and offered a little relief, but the genoa was shading the cockpit, the cold was piercing, arctic. Homer used it as an excuse to go up on deck to admire the Browning thirty-caliber machine gun, glistening in the brilliance of mid-day. Petty Officer Jackson finally surfaced through the cabin door eased himself up, squinting at the harshness of the noonday light.

Harry Coopersmith sized up the young Coast Guardsman, about the same age and size of Michael. His face was a different shape more oval than Michael's but the same look of youthful determination was there. The Coast Guardsman had darker hair but it was the same length and just as tangled.

Luther Rogers noticed Harry inspecting his warrior. "Good morning, Petty Officer Jackson. I want you to meet our new crewmember. This is Harry, Harry Coopersmith . . ."

"You must be Maxwell Jackson. I am pleased to meet you." Harry shook the limp hand.

"Uh, huh."

Max looked around the cockpit of the sailboat, trying to identify his new environment while Luther and Harry discussed him. He didn't like the sight of the horizon tilted up. He felt his head and realized that the boat was heeling. Standing, facing the chilled breeze was refreshing, but regardless, he needed to sit.

Harry offered Max a mug of coffee. "I just made it. Want milk or sugar?"

"Mm, hmm. Thank you."

Everybody in the cockpit snapped their eyes forward, their attention grabbed by a loud metallic clank. Homer offered an embarrassed smile back at them. Luther Rogers glanced at Max for his reaction. Max lifted the blue mug to his lips and took a loud sip ignoring Homer's curious exploration of the machine gun. If Max didn't appear troubled with Homer playing with the gun, then Luther Rogers wouldn't either.

"Homer, what're you doing up there? Don't shoot the mast off," Harry called forward. Homer returned to the cockpit. "I want you to teach me how to fire that machine gun." Max nodded and took another drink of his coffee.

Luther Rogers tightened the mizzen sheet, after noticing the luff. "As long as we're all here I think it proper to set up a schedule. Homer and I, and you, Harry, will take eight-hour shifts. Max should rotate through as many shifts as possible to teach us all about sinking U-boats. We can teach him to sail. Does that sound okay? Max?"

The combination of last night's whiskey and beer, and the pitching of the boat at a 15 degrees heel played a Cuban rumba in his head. Max leaned over the side and puked. He puked and puked, the vomit streamed aft. He was thankful he didn't have to stare at it or smell it, the sea carried away the unpleasantness. Max purged himself again, heaving with every muscle attached to his ribs until nothing more would come up, yet he still tried. Max heaved then relaxed and laid on the rail. He felt the bile build up and push on his throat, again he dry heaved. The fresh cool air was the only thing that kept him alive. He stared at the water unable to think. Again he heaved up nothing. He promised to himself never to drink. He suddenly could remember every drink he had swallowed, every food he had eaten, and every cigar he pretended to smoke. The cigar, again he tensed and heaved. His sides and stomach were sore. He lay on the rail, the position uncomfortable with something poking him in the ribs but was unable to muster the energy to move.

Lady's Revenge jumped over a wave. Water was rumbling down the hull and churning into white froth, he thought of the hamburger and fries, the Boston cream pie and the dill pickles he saw coming up seconds before, and the trail they left. His brain pounded as if his pulse were amplified with the swing of a hammer against the inside of his skull in unison with his heartbeat. He leaned further over the gunwale.

"Hey, diaper boy. Not going to get sick the whole patrol are ya, diaper boy. Our big warrior." Homer grunted. He wanted to learn about the machine gun. He liked the feel of the cold steel in his hands. The machine gun was a weapon that took not the strength to wield a sword, but the steadiness of good aim. Soon he would have that Nazi heart in his crosshairs. Soon he would squeeze the life out of the pumping organ, just as they had with Candice.

"How fast are we going?" Max asked not looking up from the water that was speeding down the side of the hull.

Luther Rogers was proud of his Hinckley. He threw the log overboard, a bullet shaped device with a propeller on the rear to measure ship's speed, and retrieved it as Max waited, still hanging over the side.

"Twelve knots."

Max jerked back upright, his vision blacked-out from the sudden movement.

He steadied his head in both hands until his sight returned. His eyes were alive with excitement, the older men looked on as if witnessing an epiphany, expecting to hear something profound. The Coastie gazed up at the sails; he studied the white, looming main sail, the genoa that ran past the mainmast taut, the steel running shrouds, the standing stays with telltales flying. His examination followed the luff of the mizzen sail, down the boom, the gray teak decks, the lines laid out in neat patterns on deck, the empty winch drums waiting to take halyards, the mainsheet through the tackle, the mizzen sheet where it ended in the wrinkled fist of Luther Rogers. Everyone stared at the Coast Guardsman in anticipation. Max listened.

"Is that normal?"

Luther wasn't sure what Max had meant. "Is what normal?"

"The speed?"

"Yes, sometimes faster, sometimes slower. All depends on the wind."

"Doesn't seem to be that much wind. What's her average?"

Luther picked up the logbook and did some quick arithmetic. "Maybe nine knots."

"But she'll go faster?"

Homer couldn't be a patient bystander to this game of twenty questions, "What are you getting at kid? Have you never sailed before?" Homer turned to the others, "Great, they send us some baby so we can change his diapers."

Max paused, ignoring the sarcasm, and looked at each of the old men, realizing that he might not be out of the war after all. "I didn't know that sailboats went this fast. She's fast enough to chase U-boats. And, she has something going for her that's even better than any destroyer."

Homer stared at Max's lips eagerly.

"She's silent"

The old men glanced at each other and back at Max. That was not the reaction he wanted. "Don't you get it? We're silent. We've got no engine noise. The U-boats won't know we're here. They won't be able to hear us. We can sneak right up on them!"

Luther Rogers felt his shoulders relax. He beamed with pride for this young man.

Any thoughts of ineffectual capabilities of a sailboat versus a modern man-made instrument of war eroded and galvanized his excitement. He had been starting to doubt the feasibility of the venture. Luther was not ashamed to admit his ignorance, he was learning from a kid that could be his grandchild. He felt the effect of that youthful enthusiasm draw him in like a contagious laugh around a dinner table. He was twenty again and heading into battle! His fallen tree was growing higher and higher, to the heavens.

"Hey diaper boy, can we sneak up on U-boats and shoot all the Nazis with the machine gun?"

"Mister Crown, the machine gun is not going to do us much good. The U-boats have cannons on their decks that could blow this little boat to hell and back."

Nobody aboard appreciated that last bit of information. Luther swallowed hard, he was determined not to be some old worthless man, a withering tree cleared away for the new growth.

"But with those," Max pointed toward the racks on the stern, "We can crush a U-boat up smaller than a beer can."

The roots grew deeper, reaching down into the earth, a solid foundation for Luther Rogers' tree.

Homer traded views from the Browning machine gun to the awkward looking rack in the stern. He pictured the still-pumping Nazi heart held in his hand being crushed with his own strength. Blood and tissue drained from his clenched fist. He admitted to himself that his hands were arthritic and becoming more painful each hour in the cold. The depth charge could do his work for him.

Harry thought of his son. How had Michael died? Was it painful? Had it been with a crushing bomb? He went below to prepare something for lunch.

"It's Homer's turn to fix lunch," Luther called after him.

Harry ignored him and continued down into the galley in a perfunctory daze deep in thought about his son.

With a gleam in his eye that showed his excitement Homer listened to Max, but felt something unconsciously pull at him. With great effort Homer retreated down through the hatch to join Coopersmith in the galley. "Want some help?"

"No, thank you."

"I'll take another cup of coffee, please."

Harry poured the remains of the pot into Homer's mug. "How long have your hands been bothering you?"

"You noticed? Please don't tell the others," Homer said, clenching his fist open and closed, trying to work out the pain.

Harry nodded. "I was thinking about Michael. I wish we had done so many things together, but we didn't. I was always busy." Pulling out a frying pan from the cabinet down below the sink Harry stopped with the pan dangling from his hand and turned toward Homer. "He died on Wake Atoll. It's in the Pacific," Harry said matter-of-factly.

"I'm sorry to hear that. I lost my family too," Homer said sliding into the bench seat.

Harry threw some butter into the pan and watched it sizzle, "How's about some pancakes. I've got just enough eggs. Besides it's the only thing I ever watched my wife make enough to know how."

Homer watched as Harry dumped flour and eggs into a mixing bowl and beat furiously, and then poured the lumpy paste into the pan. Watching the batter bubble Harry twirled the spatula and then flipped the pancake, he burned the first four out of nine. He did manage to make one that wasn't too bad. Setting the good one on a plate and then sliding it across the table Homer plastered a glob of butter on it, smeared it across the brown cake and covered it with syrup. Homer forced the bland and powdery substance down with sympathy.

Twenty-One

The placid water held in its grasp a sole freighter like a baby asleep on a blanket. No horizon could be discerned only the haze of a continuing sky that lay draped on the ocean's edge. A slow and deep swell moved under the surface that offered the ship a gentle rocking lullaby. A hatch swung back and forth effortlessly in an eerie, haunting solitude. The smudge that was the sun cast shadows askew on the steel, giving the ship the illusion and shape of an unfamiliar creature.

Fireman Third Class Bob Olsen sat with his head in his hands and his knees pulled up against his chest. Everything was motionless, the whole ocean waited for a breeze. The *Antarctic Penguin* rested on its side. Olsen raised his head up and surveyed the scene: the superstructure was half-submerged, the keel formed the starboard side waterline, two blades of the giant propeller rose out of the stern. Strangely, there was no debris, no bodies, only a rainbow slick of oil haloed the torpedoed hulk. But there, on the unperceived horizon, an obscure opaque form projected itself from nowhere out of the haze.

A U-boat.

Olsen gazed upon the beast without fear, nor curiosity, but relief. The sea monster offered a reprieve from the devastation that surrounded him, albeit deadly and menacing, but nonetheless an end. He was absent of any profound thought, the trauma he had endured for the last five hours had left him incapable of nothing more than a desire for conclusion. The blank stare, the mesmerizing effect swallowed him. Olsen watched the object in the water as it maneuvered.

And then, it was gone.

Now, he was totally, absolutely alone.

Kaptinleutnant Fulmer surfaced to spy his catch. He held the freighter in the binoculars view. Always cautious, Fulmer scanned the points of the compass for the enemy. He raised the binoculars back to his eyes. A white object, just discernible, traveled the edge of his visibility. He couldn't identify predator or prey. Fulmer studied the contact. It was a sailboat. A sailboat was not worth the ammunition, nor worth the threat of being spotted.

The beast, its skin closed tight and cold, slid back down into its domain. The still tranquil Atlantic swallowed the sea monster, accepting it back into its bosom.

Twenty-Two

The stars shown bright and the crisp night air felt rejuvenating on Luther's face as he breathed in the saltiness of the sea. Luther closed his eyes and ran his fingers through his thinning mat of silver. The creaks and groans of *Lady's Revenge*: music. Slowly he turned aft to where Homer sat in the cockpit waiting to be relieved. They had been at sea for some time now. The crew was taking shape, the routine becoming routine, and Max making progress in his lessons toward becoming a great sailor and navigator.

The compass light illuminated his shipmate. "Homer, is everything okay? You have that thousand mile stare." Luther asked.

Luther could see a tear form in the man's lower eyelid, but Homer squinted his eyes shut and wiped his palms into his eyes before the tears could fall. Luther leaned down and sat next to Homer, placing his gloved hand on the wheel, "I can relieve you now. It looks like we'll be able to get a great celestial fix this morning. Should we have the kid do it?" When Homer didn't reply Luther continued, "Why don't you go below and get some sleep."

Homer silently retreated through the hatch to the saloon. Sirius left a silver finger of reflection across the Atlantic, Luther watched the shadows of the passing waves dance under the star until he felt himself become rapt as if by Sirens. He laughed at the mythological analogy and did his thirty-minute ritual: check the sail trim, compass, speed, scan the entire ocean for contacts, and finally make the log entry. When the rising sun started to show evidence of its arrival, Luther set the autopilot and snuck below to wake Max.

Luther was back at the controls when Max stumbled out of the hatchway rubbing his eyes. "What time is it, sir? Feels like oh-dark-thirty."

"Good morning, Max. Thought it may be good for you to take the morning fix."

Despite his being awakened from a great dream with an unidentified brunette, Max shook himself awake with a stretch and anticipated the opportunity to learn the ancient craft. He was fascinated by the art of navigation, something that he never did in his rate. The quartermasters and officers navigated, as a Sonarman his job was to detect and kill submarines, preferably German.

"Here, now try to bring Sirius down to the horizon."

Max took the sextant from Luther and sighted in the star. He slowly moved the sextant arm and lowered the device, restarting three times after the star disappeared from view. Finally, he was able to set the star on the almost discernable dark line of the horizon. "Mark."

"Make sure it's at the very lowest point if you pivot the sextant around the star. Max did as he was instructed and saw that he had missed the lower limb, again he barked out, "Mark."

Luther wrote down the time, "Now get another one."

Max went through the process for four more stars and then replaced the sextant in the velvet padded wooden box on the cockpit bench. "Do you remember how I showed you to reduce these into lines?"

Max nodded and went below to begin the calculations. Luther smiled at his pupil like a proud father. He could not remember a time where he felt more alive; moreover, that sensation of being young once again ran through his veins like the waters from the fountain of youth. He spent the remainder of the watch bathed in satisfaction. By the time his watch ended the fog rolled in like some dark ubiquitous creature and Luther could not see more than a hundred yards in any direction. Harry blew the steam from his coffee mug as he climbed out of the saloon hatch. Suddenly, the energy seemed to be sapped out of Luther at the sight of his relief.

Harry simply grabbed the wheel and nodded. Max suddenly ran up the ladder, "I've got our position. Came out like a pinwheel, maybe not a perfect pinwheel but I'm pretty confident we're right here." Max pointed at the pencil mark on the chart that flapped in the wind.

"Well done. Might amount to something after all," Harry said with a warm smile.

With a pat on Max's shoulder Luther offered a small grin of accomplishment in response and then retreated to his bed below, the fountain of youth missed a few veins as his seventy-one-year-old body ached and longed for the warmth of his berth.

A quick scan of the horizon revealed that the fog was rising. Max sat across from Harry Coopersmith. They were both tired of conversation so sat in silence and listened to the creaks and moans of the sailboat. Harry eased off the wheel a little to bring *Lady* back on course. The light sails were up, two fore sails, the main and mizzen. The leeward standing rigging shroud snapped with no weight to bear. The mizzen was not staying full, Harry got up and hauled on the mizzen boomvang, the small block and tackle device used to prevent the horizontal spar from suddenly becoming a vertical spar and ripping the sail.

The water ended in a haze near the sky's edge as the sun rose and developed into a bright smudge in an imprecise sky. The boredom was laborious. Harry held out a pack of Wrigley's

"No thanks," Max said as he sipped down more coffee.

Harry unwrapped a piece of gum and stuck it in his mouth. Harry didn't talk much lately Max noticed, but at this hour nobody did. Harry sat in a state somewhere between consciousness and cognition; it was one of the few moments that Michael did not consume his thoughts. Contemplating the next meal, Harry mentally inventoried the remaining stores. If the crew had had any misgiving about Harry's late arrival they were extinguished with his eagerness to take over the mess chores. He had never cooked, but somehow it came instinctively—watching Patty cook for twenty-three years had had an effect.

"What's that?" Max pointed off the port quarter.

Harry turned to see where Max's finger aimed. "I don't see anything . . . Wait, yeah."

Max squinted through the binoculars. "Damn, I lost it."

"There." Harry pointed, but then he too lost the image. It appeared to be a light shadow of a vessel. He strained to refocus. It was gone. "Could it be a U-boat?"

"I suppose, but if it were it would surely see us also. They'd have better lookouts than us. If it was its long gone. It'd take us a couple hours just to get over there. Should we tell Luther and Homer?"

"I don't think it'd make much difference . . . maybe Luther, but Homer is able to make a big deal about it."

Max thought of what Homer would say about the diaper boy not going after a contact. Too chicken, he'd say. No, Harry was right, Max settled back into his still warm position.

Harry Coopersmith ran through the inventory again. Maybe use up the rest of the Spam, fry it up with the canned pineapple. Next patrol he would buy the stores, powdered milk and flour were a must and try to get some canned fruit that would sweeten the meal a bit. He had had no opportunity to use the Hinckley's oven thus far, maybe he could have Patty give him some recipes for cake or a casserole.

He planned a big feast in his thoughts for the next patrol.

The wind picked up, pulling him out of his culinary daydream.

"Max, go forward and haul in the genoa. Then get ready to bring up the heavier mains'l and mizzen."

As he maneuvered over the lines running strategically across the deck Max noticed a plume of dark smoke from the direction of the sighting. He froze trying to adjust his focus. "U-BOAT! U-boat. All hands on deck!" He quickly ran back to the cockpit and met Homer and Luther there. "Homer get the thirty ready, Luther better take the helm." Max turned to Harry, "Help me get the depth charges ready for attack." An electricity of excitement sparked the air. Homer pushed two green ammo boxes out through the foredeck hatch and then reappeared out on deck. "Luther, I'll crew your foresails."

"Ready to come about?" Luther called out, "Hard-a-lee" as he spun the wheel the large Hinckley crossed the wind and the ketch began to pick up speed.

"Ouch," Harry called out, and then lifted his hand from between the metal level and the depth charge. He kissed the backside of his knuckles, more startled than hurt.

"Watch out for the arm level. Better dial in for fifty feet. Port fifty, check. Pull the launch arm to unlock position. Air pressure green," Max read through the check-off list for depth charges. "Now starboard side."

Harry quickly slid to the starboard side along with Max. "Got it, fifty. Unlock, check. Air pressure green, check," Harry barked.

Max and Harry dropped down into the cockpit. With a pair of binoculars Max stood to judge the distance to the U-boat. He could barely make out the conning tower, but the diesel exhaust left a dark tail that wafted into the now clear morning sky. Instinctively, Max scanned the horizon for other contacts. He noticed a heavy black cloud rise from the southern horizon. He scanned back to the U-boat. "Shit, he's going after a merchant ship."

"I don't see any other ships, Max"

"Right there, Luther," Max pointed to the exhaust from a coal burner. "He's below the horizon. They haven't seen us, not even looking behind themselves." Max looked up the sails, "Can we go faster?"

"I've got her as close to the wind as I dare," Luther said.

Harry had the other binoculars and was watching the U-boat intently. "It looks like we're gaining." He lowered the glasses, "Do you think we'll beat them to the merchant, Luther?"

"Take the helm, Harry and I'll get the log. Max, get a bearing on the merchant and the U-boat and I'll try to calculate the rate of closure."

Max did as he was told, pulled the sextant out and started to dial in the angle between the two contacts, but called after Luther as he went below, "How are you going to do that?"

Luther reappeared, "Geometry, son. It's a simple calculation using trigonometry tables."

The wind was stalling. The merchant ship was now entirely visible as it came closer to *Lady's Revenge* and the U-boat. Max readjusted the angle on the sextant between the two contacts and called out the numbers quickly and then brought the scope back to his eye to readjust. "I calculate about twenty minutes or so the U-boat will be close enough to fire a torpedo. Where is it now? I've lost it." Luther said.

"It's submerging," Max said, slumping back down onto the upholstered bench.

"What if we warned the merchant ship on the wireless radio?" Harry offered.

"Why didn't I think of that?" Max ran down through the hatch. He quickly flipped the transmit button, "All merchant ships in vicinity of. . ." Max ran his finger from the position he plotted earlier toward the New Jersey shoreline, "Point Pleasant. Thirty miles offshore Point Pleasant, New Jersey. This is Coast Guard six-five-three-two-zero, we are in sight of a German U-boat in our location, thirty miles due east of Point Pleasant, New Jersey. Please respond all vessels in this vicinity." Max waited, nothing. He called out again and again on the three different frequencies that might be monitored by the merchant fleet. Still nothing.

"Any luck down there?"

"NO! What's the U-boat doing?" Max reemerged. "Why aren't we going after them!"

Luther pulled on the mainsheet, "Sorry, the wind doesn't seem to share our enthusiasm."

The merchant freighter was plainly visible at a range of about five miles. Luther couldn't make out the U-boat anymore but he watched with anticipation as the freighter progressed north unaware of the danger that lurked below the surface. The gentle ting of the shroud beating against the mast was heard as the men looked on. Expectedly, a small light appeared starboard side amidships on the freighter. Suddenly, a fireball rose just aft of the first hit, it was followed by a dull thwap sound. The freighter came to a stop and slowly rolled toward them. They sat and watched from the safety of *Lady's Revenge* for the next three hours as the ship burned and finally sank below the waves. Fire dotted the surface of the ocean marking the site of the grave. Luther and Homer managed to make slow progress with a whisper of wind. "Any one hungry, I'll go make lunch," Harry said, going below.

Max just stared as the debris came closer.

"Go to the foc's'l with the boat hook to push the crap out of the way. Let's see if we can find any survivors," Homer said.

"Aye, aye."

Max sat with his legs dangling over the rail and shoved what little debris there was out of the path of the sailboat. He didn't see bodies, no survivors; surprisingly, nothing that was distinguishable save for a scorched teddy bear.

Twenty-Three

"You must always remember one thing, if you don't remember anything else..."

Homer impatiently retorted, "I remember already. You probably forgot. How do we kill the damn Nazi Bastards? Check the spacing and the firing pin slide, yeah, yeah. Hey diaper boy, are you a virgin with this gun? Ever killed anybody?"

"Mister Crown, the only one that's going to get killed is you if you don't take this seriously. That's for the Browning, this is a depth charge launcher," Max said, pointing to the machine gun and then slapped his hand on the side of the K-gun depth charge launcher.

"Homer, please," Luther Rogers said with an exasperated glare.

"I'm sorry, diaper boy. Please go on."

Max continued, obviously irritated by Homer, "Open the cover like this," the round bowl hinged open. "And then unscrew the breech to insert the cartridge. . ." Max held up on of the small explosive charges and inserted it into the chamber of the K-gun. "When you trigger the gun, here, it fires off the cartridge and releases the gases into the expansion chamber, out the amber, and finally sends the Mark VI depth charge toward the damned Hun." Max slapped the depth charge, "this is the older Mark VI depth charge with only three hundred pounds of TNT. Always remember to set the depth and launch angle so that the depth charge is off at a safe distance. If the depth charge were to be dropped over the side with a shallow depth dialed in the thing would blow *Lady's Revenge* to smithereens."

"I'm going below to start dinner." Harry muttered as he thought of his son. Had he been blown to smithereens? He could not, did not, want to imagine the fate of his son. But, masochistically, his imagination invented every horrible, conceivable manner to maim a human body. The thought of Michael on some island in the Pacific fighting for his life occupied every conscious hour. He found cooking comforting, therapeutic.

"Hey, diaper boy, what about the machine gun?"

"You really want to kill, don't you?" Max retorted.

Homer gave Max a scornful glare. It was true, he was consumed with passion for killing. Revenge meant everything to him. His sense of warmth was growing colder each day. His skin was metamorphosing into cold blue gun steel. Homer would not return to feel the pleasures of living until he had rung the life out of every Nazi shit-heel. "Just do your job. Teach me to shoot the machine gun. If you don't I have alternative instruments. I have my rifle below, and this." Homer gripped the .454 Colt.

"Mister Crown, you better be careful with that. If it went off in your holster, that thing would blow a hole through the boat, or worse kill one of us."

Luther didn't like the sight of that huge caliber pistol hanging off Homer's belt any more than anyone else on board, but he tolerated it because he knew Homer Crown.

Max and Homer continued to argue. "Listen, I know how to use this thing." He maintained but Max wasn't satisfied.

Max glanced back at Luther with a what-do-I-do-about-this-guy look. Luther Rogers read Max's face. "Don't worry Petty Officer Jackson, Homer doesn't dare load it."

Max smirked.

KABANG! The report sang out. Harry poked his head out of the hatch.

Homer re-holstered the Colt.

"Homer, don't be an asshole. I want that thing unloaded on my boat!"

"How do you fire this damn machine-gun you little urchin," Homer demanded.

Harry turned, making his way back down to the saloon below, "We're getting a little cabin fever out here. We better go in soon," He said to no one in particular.

Luther was surprised by Homer's outrage. The man was normally harmless, he thought, but this was someone he had never seen before. It was time to go back in and get a reality check. Luther was afraid that Homer may not possess the mental facilities to make the next voyage—the war and his personal loss may have finally put him over the edge, and Luther hated to admit it, his age. He would have to look for someone else if Homer continued on his present course to insanity.

While Max and Homer where quarreling over the Browning water-cooled thirty Luther saw a strange dark object floating up ahead. "Max, what is that off the starboard bow?"

Max looked under the shade of his hand. "I don't know. Shall we go see?"

Homer eyed the floating thing and secretly hoped it was the bloated corpse of a Nazi.

Harry surfaced out of the cabin to see what had everyone's attention. He lowered himself down next to Luther in the cockpit.

"Not another one. The bastards got another one," Homer said out loud.

Luther let out some mainsheet and aimed the boat toward the strange target. He noticed a sheen of oil on the surface, then more debris. Pieces of wood, milled and undamaged floated by. A wicker chair, upright as if waiting for someone to sit bobbed up and down. More debris littered their path. Looking down at what he knew were the remains of a torpedoed vessel, Luther Rogers was painted with the same sensation that had swept through him that night at Sandy Hook. He was looking into an open grave.

If he had lost one ounce of certitude, with Homer going berserk, Harry lost in memories of his son, and Max pure, cunning, and innocent, it all was suddenly restored to its formidable self. Luther knew he didn't have the resolution of Harry, or the vengeance of Homer to fuel his quest. His was more subtle, an act of preservation.

More debris drifted by. A form brushed against the slow moving *Lady*, it rolled in the wake. All eyes were transfixed on the mass. Luther Rogers let out a small sigh as he recognized the deformed face of a man. Only black sockets remained where the eyes had been eaten away, small fish swarmed around the underside and fingertips. The enlarged corpse strained a Lieutenant Merchant Marine uniform. Luther contemplated retrieving the body but couldn't bring himself to touch the decaying carcass. The rest of the crew watched the body float ominously by.

The timeless pause cast a shadow over the boat. Luther finally heard Max and Homer start arguing again about the machine gun, the ship righted itself back to normalcy. Harry retreated to the galley, thinking about his son rotting away in the Pacific with crabs crawling in and out of his empty sockets. Luther tasted a sour feeling in his stomach. He could turn the Hinckley back toward Long Beach and escape from all this. Was it deliberate and self-defeating to put himself through this kind of horror and maltreatment?

Luther was introducing himself to alcohol at McSorley's when the Philippine War troops came home. Two of the soldiers were seated across the dark pub. Mustering up the courage, Luther walked over to ask them what it was like. He approached their table and asked the stupid question. They were drunk and unkind, they accused him of cowardice. His pride was forever tarnished, that one-legged solider from the train station had been brave.

Luther, well past fighting age, could sit out the war in the warmth of his own home. But in doing that he would never know the answer to his question. It was not something you ask anybody except for yourself. Was he just patronizing himself with this grand adventure? Turn the boat around. Luther digested the sight of the dead sailor like a cinder block in his gut.

This was why he was out here. To try and stop the senseless carnage. Luther pulled in the mainsheet and raced off, putting as much distance between him and the debris as the wind would allow.

Twenty-Four

It was the morning of their planned return. The first patrol demonstrated how unprepared they really were—food stores were ill-planned, the sea air was colder than they remembered, the wireless couldn't warn the freighter, one stinking sighting, the horrible evidence of U-boat activity that littered the ocean, and the only survivor was a bloated body.

"Everybody topside!" Homer called.

Max was the first to appear. Harry Coopersmith followed him. Luther Rogers had just finished his watch two hours prior and was slow to surface out of the warmth below. The wind had picked up. Luther heard the water rushing past the hull as he made his way topside.

"What is it Mister Crown?"

"Get the spinnaker ready. We're on a down wind leg, should be down wind the whole way back to Point Lookout,"

Homer described the navigable cut between Jones Beach and Long Beach.

Land was visible but Luther couldn't make out any of the landmarks of Long Island. He was tired and his eyesight always suffered in that condition. Even with his glasses on the land was a fuzzy mass off in the distance.

"Come on Max," Harry said, walking forward with a bundle of sail.

"Want me get the spinnaker pole?"

"Yes, please. You're making a first-rate sailor," Luther encouraged him.

Luther took the sail from Harry. Harry and Max would be stronger to hoist the sail. The halyard hook was lowered to Luther; he found the wire peak of the spinnaker and clipped the hook. Next he had to make sure the sheath was set correctly, the ripcord was untangled and ready to go up. Max stood ready at the handle on the mainmast winch. The spinnaker halyard was wrapped twice around the drum, Harry stood aft ready to haul. Luther rechecked the deck lines to see that all was clear. He put the whisker pole in the mast notch and readied it to fit in the fore corner of the new sail.

"We all ready?" Luther asked.

"Aye, Captain," Harry called out.

"Haul away you rolling kings!" Luther began to sing,

In South Australia I was born
Heave away, Haul away
In South Australia 'round Cape Horn
Bound for South Australia
Haul away you rolling kings
Heave away, Haul away
All the day you'll hear me sing
I'm bound for South Australia

Harry hauled, leaning back against the weight of the halyard. Max spun the winch handle. Slowly the spinnaker rose off the deck. Luther ran the sheets through the guides and tied figure eights in the bitter ends to prevent them running away. The green sheath was now erect along the forward shroud. Luther put the rip cord through a block and handed it to Max who had just made fast the spinnaker halyard on a mast cleat. Harry ran aft with the ripcord and dropped down into the cockpit with Homer. The sail, white, light, and oversized, snapped open. The whisker pole rose above and paralleled the deck at about four feet. The green sheath was crumpled and odd looking at the top of the sail. *Lady's Revenge* picked up speed from the extra sail area.

"Let go the jib sheet and ease the halyard."

"Aye, aye. Mister Rogers, which one is the jib halyard?" Max asked

"The forward cleat. Put it on the winch and lower it slowly. Harry, can you help?"

Harry came forward, stepping over the sheets and deck lines carefully. The jib was lowered much too fast, Harry and Luther struggled to keep it from the water. They grabbed handfuls of sail and pulled it to their bosom, as if to see who could get the most sail in his arms. Finally, the halyard was on deck and secured. The sail was stuffed into a bag and dropped down the hatch into the sail locker aft of the chain locker for the anchor.

Luther felt his shoulder and hands, the chronic pain incumbent with old age. He was sore and tired and relieved to be going in. "I think I'm going to take a quick nap," Luther announced. He retreated down to his rack and instantly fell sound asleep.

Harry followed quickly below to clean up the mess left from breakfast in the galley.

"You going to get drunk this time?" Homer asked.

"Sorry, Mister Crown, that we didn't get to sink any U-boats."

Homer ignored the apology, "You got pretty sauced last time in, throwing chunks all over the Atlantic."

The thought instantly made Max remember the rotten, asphalt taste.

Homer smiled in mock amusement, he looked up at the sails and adjusted the trim slightly, if nothing more than to reassert himself. She was making ten knots he figured. They would be back in soon. "Listen Max, I want a U-boat bad. I want to kill the goddamn Nazi bastards with my bare hands." Homer looked down at his hands, they were swollen and throbbing with pain. Had anyone else noticed? "Next trip. If those things back there really work I'd be happy to stuff one up some Hun's ass. Aye, but we had a good patrol." Homer gazed back to seaward, "I have a feeling it's going to be a long war."

Max couldn't believe it. Homer had called him Max not Diaper Boy. "I wonder what's been happening in Europe, or the Pacific? Being out here for twenty days without news really is the worst. We could've lost the war for all we know."

Homer spied the sails again and adjusted the mainsheet slightly and then hauled on the port spinnaker sheet. "And I suppose the radio calls are from Nazi impostors?"

Max shifted in his seat, Homer was his least favorite of the old men to stand watch. Max had not acquired the taste for Homer's practiced art of sarcasm.

"Mister Crown. . ." Max started but could think of no conversation, he let the words fade.

"Well, spit it out diaper boy."

Discipline, Max told himself.

They sat in silence.

Max finally broke, "What'd you think when we saw that dead body? I've never seen a dead body before. Except for my uncle Albert, he was in a casket so that was different. You're old, you ever think about dying?"

Homer paused, it was something he avoided. Of course it was a question he often had contemplated, especially at his age, but he tried to piece together his response. He turned to face Jackson and began. "The only greatness is found in death. Life has too many falsehoods, complications and decorations. The only time a person is complete, as complete as they ever shall be, is at that moment of death. It is at that precise moment that one will be at the pinnacle—all the fibers that make up his convictions shall be exposed. It will come as a deliverance . . . What other moment in life is so pure?"

Max opened his marlinspike knife blade and dug the dirt out from under his nails; he wasn't sure how to answer the question, nor if he should at all. He left the answer to the question suspended in the morning air of the small cockpit like a strange odor.

Homer was acutely aware of the awkwardness that was draped over the conversation. "Stop picking at your nails. That's not polite. Do I have to teach you everything? Why don't you go down below to see if one of the others can powder you or wash you up."

Luther was awake after a quick 30-minute nap and sitting at the chart table scrutinizing a portion of the ocean that was south of their position. The first patrol had produced nothing, except disappointment, and a test of patience and endurance against their greater enemy: boredom. Luther looked up at the figure that blocked the morning light into the cabin. Max craned his head down into the opening, smiled and disappeared, being replaced by the light.

Max sat back down on the cockpit bench next to Homer. "They're both awake."

"Even Luther?"

"Yeah, but he looks really dog-tired."

Homer glanced at Max, sized him up as if for the first time, and offered the sheet lines. "Take the ship, diaper boy. If you don't sink us or hit anything I'll make you my cabin boy," Homer said. He was glad to be returning to land. It was not that he longed for shore like a seasick Irish farmer escaping the potato famine on his passage across the Atlantic; but nonetheless, there was something exciting about land, that undeniable, attraction, like a beautiful woman. Despite the desire to come home to solid ground, Homer was closer, spiritually, to his own being when he was at sea than at any other time.

Max sat up from his slouch and greedily took the lines and caressed them—the soft double braid felt alive. He looked down at his hands, smiled at cotton rope, then up at the sails, finally, out ahead of the boat and felt that same sensation of a first kiss. He was in charge of the boat. He was making the damn thing go! He pulled in the mizzen sail an inch or two just to affirm his new authority.

"I'm going down below to warm up and get something to eat for breakfast. Harry owes me three dollars over last night's cribbage game, maybe I'll let him win it back. Can you handle it, diaper boy?"

"Yes," Max said not to acknowledge his ability but in a manner that a Captain granted permission.

"That's a Samson double braid line, not your dick. So be careful how you handle it."

Max pried the main sheet out of the clam cleat to test the strength of the boat. He was astonished at the force pulling at the line. He could not hold it. The sheet slipped, the main boom swung outward further. *Lady* offered a subtle snap in reaction, Max immediately pushed the line down into the spring-loaded clam cleat, hoping no one down below noticed.

"Watch it! Trim 'er up," Homer's voice called from down below, his hopes denied.

He steered off and quickly hauled the boom back in. Once again the boat was heeled and slicing through the small chop. With his new command bubble popped, Max sat nervously on the edge of the cockpit bench spying on and off between the sails and compass. How much further to land, how long would he have to concentrate? Max started to feel the pain of concentration in his eyes and the forward part of his head—these old men made it look so easy.

"How much further?" Max called down through the hatch.

"About six or seven hours," a voice grumbled from the cabin.

Max slouched in his green Coast Guard issued foul-weather jacket, 'six or seven hours' he whispered to himself.

Down in the cabin, bright mahogany paneling offered most of the color. Blue drapes and cushions on the foldaway rack and table benches were the only other contrast to the reddish brown woodwork. Forward, through the closed door, Max and Harry shared a queen-sized V-berth. They had a head and sink and two small narrow closets. Max had put most of his belongings in the storage hammocks, while Harry preferred the under-rack drawers. Aft were two staterooms assigned to Luther and Homer that were adjoined by a common head with a shower. As the four settled into at-sea life, each took possession of a little real estate—Luther preferred the chart table, Homer the wrap-around bench behind the galley table, Harry had made the galley his favorite spot but would cram into any open seat, and Max faced aft on the galley bench, preferring to see out the hatch to the cockpit. Harry had redone the galley to suit his needs; pots, pans, and utensils were rearranged and the spices moved from the left cabinet to the right—little subtleties that made all the difference in the world.

Homer sat across from Harry at the galley table on the port side, playing cribbage. Luther was hunched over, asleep at the navigator's desk on the aft starboard side. Harry cursed at a cribbage hand, throwing his cards down on the table while Homer cringed at the loss of eleven points. Luther raised his head and looked toward the excitement.

"Sorry, Luther," Harry said.

"It's okay. I should go lay down." He watched them play, not wanting to go to his rack. Luther gazed at Homer with sympathetic eyes, he wondered if Homer should make the next patrol—the arthritic hands had swelled, making it difficult to even look at him, and his sarcasm had verged on dementia. They all made great effort to not notice. Sanguine and despairing, Luther made no decision concerning the fate of his friend but instead closed his eyes and rested his head back on his folded arms. He knew Homer was determined with an unparalleled Nazi-killing doggedness. His friend had little reason for life, that Luther couldn't argue. Besides, strength had nothing to do with fighting the enemy, an enemy he was convinced they would never see, as long as Homer had the strength to pull the trigger or hold the helm. Luther attempted to convince himself of Homer's contribution to his crew. It was not in his authority to deprive Homer of sailing around in boredom. He would surely die if denied the Corsair Fleet.

Luther couldn't sleep so he went topside. He sat across the cockpit admiring the young warrior as Max constantly scanned the deck hardware and sails like somebody taking a driver's test. The kid had the look of fortitude etched across his thin face that Luther admired. Max would have admitted it was nervousness. Black wavy hair swirled around his head and a dark growth covered his chin that made him look older, more rugged—this was the brave warrior Luther had always wanted to be but was deprived by the circumstances in life. Luther scratched his own three-week growth, shaving a luxury *Lady's Revenge* could not afford, and wondered if maybe he looked as impressive.

Max continued to concentrate on the sails, checking and correcting the luff; it was becoming exhausting.

"We should all go out together some night in port," Luther offered.

Max glanced over at the man who looked tired and wrinkled and old. Max thought the suggestion was instinctive, something he would have never thought to mention. It was an unspeakable invitation aboard every ship that he ever sailed, a tradition from days when a sailor's passage was a risky venture and dictated that all the crew celebrate the safe voyage. Why should he have thought otherwise? No one, not wives, friends, or lovers can understand the ordeals suffered at sea— only shipmates make worthy drinking partners.

"I expected no less. Is Homer going to play Tom Mix with his six-gun when we go?"

Luther Rogers smiled and then chuckled at the thought.

Twenty-Five

Homer and Luther piloted the sailboat into the harbor as Harry and Max fulfilled their roles as crewmen. Just as he stuffed the jib in the bag for storage Max noticed a woman standing on the dock. Soft blonde hair billowed across her face. She stood in brown pumps with tan silk stockings that wrapped shapely legs, reassuring the world there was a God. A red belt encircled her small waist and a white sweater clung to her curves. The light khaki skirt flapped like a luffing sail. She reached up and pulled back a stray strand of hair. Max saw the icy green eyes even from this distance—he never saw such intense color.

"Quite a looker, eh?" Harry whispered in his ear.

Absentmindedly, Max pulled down the mainsail as he assessed the woman. He didn't take his eyes off her until she looked at him and smiled. With an embarrassed grin he quickly refocused on the sail, but his eyes had a will of their own and slowly traveled back to the god-sent creature. The white teeth formed a perfect smile, she waved. "Grandpapa, welcome home. Nana sent me down here with some cakes." She offered up a pink box.

"Oh, Louise, I didn't expect you to come all this way. How did you get here?" Luther asked.

"Greetings, Louise," Homer waved.

"Mister Crown," Louise nodded. "I have dad's Buick. I'm staying at the Atlantic Beach house for break. Thought I'd do some school work, get a jump start on next semester's classes."

Max stored the sails and then jumped to the dock to get a bucket and scrub-brush from the utility locker. He smelled her, a combination of soap, perfume, and cinnamon donuts—it was a fragrance, no a potion. She was a little shorter than Max, about a hundred pounds wet, he figured. Even her fingernail polish was a perfect red. The radiance of her beauty seemed to suck him in—as if the laws of physics were at play, pulling him by some unexplained gravitational force. He knocked the bucket clear of the other gear stored in the locker and threw the swab into it. A water spigot attached to side of the storage locker protruded far enough that Max, with his thoughts on the girl, knocked his chin. He slid the bucket under the faucet, adjusted the galvanized receptacle with his foot, and then turned the valve, but that unexplained force pulled at him. Under his arm that he used to prop himself up against small storage building Max twisted his head to admire her, hoping she didn't notice his clumsy display.

Suddenly Louise looked at him, he immediately turned away as nonchalantly as possible. She said with a smile, "Your water's spilling everywhere."

Max quickly turned off the faucet. If he could, he would have shrunk to a size of cockroach and crawl under the bucket of water. He hefted the bucket and retreated to the boat for the post-sail wash avoiding her gaze. Even her voice was that of an angel. As he pushed the stiff bristle brush across the deck he stole another glance in her direction and watched as she retrieved a silver case from her handbag and withdrew a cigarette. He didn't smoke, but for her he would gladly take up the habit. Tapping the end against the silver case she approached the sailboat and then leaned toward him for a light.

"Sorry, I don't."

Louise smiled at him. He felt weightless, the swelling in his chest felt as if it would take his breath. "It's quite a nasty habit, but I do enjoy it nonetheless. Mostly when I'm on break from school," she said returning the cigarette to the case. "Which alumni do you affiliate yourself with?"

"He's my executive officer, second in command of *Lady*," Luther came to his rescue.

Max looked into those green eyes as if he were Icarus drawn to the heights, "I didn't go to college. I joined up instead."

"How romantic," she said as she brushed her hand on his arm.

Frozen with elation, Max looked down at the spot where the green-eyed mythological creature touched him. "My name is Max," he stammered.

"Louise, pleased to meet you." Her hand was warm and soft as a chamois cloth. "Are you staying with grandpapa at the Atlantic Beach house?"

"Louise," Max whispered under his breath. He swallowed hard and said, "No, I'm sleeping on board." Suddenly realizing he was still holding her, he withdrew his hand and stuffed it into his pocket as though he were afraid the sensation of her touch would be lost if exposed to the air.

Louise turned to Luther and said, "Oh, nonsense. Grandpapa, please let's all stay at the Atlantic Beach house."

Max noticed that Luther was as powerless as he felt to resist the potency of this goddess. "I've got to finish cleaning up."

"Very well, it was such a pleasure to meet you, Max. Get some of the cakes before these old cronies eat them all. I look forward to hearing about your adventures tonight," Louise said. She pulled the cigarette back out and lit it as she walked back down the dock toward the blue Buick that was parked up on the seawall. Max admired the sway of the khaki skirt as it retreated back to the heavens.

"She's a nice girl, just a little too sassy, like her mother," Luther said into his ear.

"Yes, sir. I mean...I didn't mean. . ."

"Attractive though. It's quite alright, Max. I would be disappointed if she didn't solicit a reaction from you," Luther patted him on the back, the physical demonstration more powerful than any expression of affection he could have articulated in speech.

"I'll swab the decks," Max said trying to escape the conversation with her grandfather. "Luther, could you have Homer clean the thirty?" Max asked. "That's one job he'll probably enjoy."

Lady's Revenge was soon spotless in a dull grey sort of way, but she was ship-shape and disinfected.

Harry was the last to finish when he appeared from the galley.

"What do you say we go to Filthy McNasty's for a drink? Harry?"

"I'm in," Luther said. Harry nodded agreement. Max stood as they all looked at him. Why couldn't they just go to the damned Atlantic Beach house and drink with Louise? "Filthy McNasty's, with a name like that it sounds ideal for us," Max said but he wanted to scream, 'What the hell is wrong with the Atlantic Beach house?'

Collin McGrady's, or Filthy McNasty's, as it was known by the locals, experienced a boom with the workers from Grumman coming down every Thursday through Sunday night. Soldiers, Sailors, and Marines on leave before going overseas came in to have a last drink with their fathers. An unusually large tavern, Filthy McNasty's occupied a block on the waterfront of the quiet Long Island village. It had seven pool tables, a row of eleven booths, six four-top tables, and a jukebox that played the big bands. The thirty-foot bar fronted a mirror that was warped and sagged from age. It was early, so the Grumman crowd had not yet arrived to blow the paychecks they got for the first time since the lean years of the Depression. Peanut shucks littered the floor. The employees used the excuse that it added to the character of the place. A large barrel at the end of the bar was filled each evening; customers helped themselves, filling straw baskets.

Harry returned to the table with two baskets full.

". . . I was sitting in the cockpit and suddenly, bang," Max said, retelling the story with three beers of lubrication to aid him along.

"Yeah, I was standing right there," Harry said, setting the peanuts down, and using his pointer finger as the barrel showing how close Homer had been. "I thought he'd shot my ear off."

Homer showed slight embarrassment but laughed along with the rest of them. Luther snorted in mid-chuckle, couldn't help himself as tears rolled down his cheeks. That got more laughs around the table. The guffaw finally arrived at a lull when Homer raised his glass, "To those poor bastards on the freighter." The toast sobered them instantly.

Harry held up his drink and added to himself, to the Marines on Wake, and Michael.

The *Lady's Revenge* crew gently set their glasses back down on the table.

Harry broke the silence "Did you see Max stumbling all over himself at the sight of Luther's granddaughter?" said with a chuckle.

Homer added, "He looked more nervous than a long-tailed cat in a room full of rocking chairs." And that brought back the merriment.

Suddenly, four sailors walked in with a bang as one of them knocked over a chair, already drunk their boisterous arrival announced them to the McNasty's crowd. The *Lady's* men turned back toward each other as the sailors settled into a table across the room.

"I guess I've got to call you cabin boy now, instead of diaper boy. Seein' how you got us back in without sinking or running aground."

"I thought I was doing pretty damned good sailing the boat. . ." Max giggled, the fourth beer taking its toll, "then I let the main sheet go. Gosh, I couldn't believe how hard it was to hold it." Max finished his Genny Ale. "I've got respect for you old guys sailing those yachts. I always thought it was a lazy sport. Tell me, Mister Homer, ha, ha. Mister Homer. . .

Mister Crown, tell me about the America's Cup."

"Don't get him started the night's not long enough," Luther said with an exaggerated groan.

"Shut up Luther, if the diaper boy wants to know about the America's Cup, I'll tell 'em."

"Mister Crown, I thought I got promoted?"

"Huh?" Homer replied.

Harry got up with the empty glasses, "Max, another?"

Harry slowed as he walked past the sailors. "Can I get you men something to drink?"

The smallest one spoke up first, "Damn straight, get us fighting men a drink." The quiet one reminded him of Michael. He thought of Michael sitting in some saloon somewhere drinking with his fellow Marines.

Harry paid for the sailors' round and his own four beers. He returned to the table with two mugs in each hand and then went back for another basket of peanuts.

Some of the Grumman employees started to drift in.

"Excuse me, Mister Rogers," Max said pushing himself up onto his unsteady feet. "My molars are floatin' I've got to take a piss. I knew this guy on the cutter that said that holding your piss until you were about to burst, and finally going was better than sex."

"You've got allot to learn about sex, kid. Go already." Luther shook his head, "Give the cabin boy a few beers, can't shut him up." Luther watched protectively as Max swerved through the maze of tables toward the restroom behind the dartboard. Smiling with pride, Luther turned back around, lifted the fresh mug of lager and took a sip. He couldn't remember when a beer had tasted better.

Harry pried open a shell and sent the peanut flying into Homer's suds. The three crewmembers exploded into laughter.

Across the bar Max felt better and dried his hands on the back of his trousers as he started back for his shipmate's table. "Hey, kid!" A voice called above the jukebox, playing Makin' Whoopee.

A sailor was motioning for him so Max turned left instead of right around a four-top table with Grumman workers, toward the sailors.

Luther jumped up when he saw the sailors getting up to taunt Max. The big one pushed Max back into an empty booth. Racing forward across the shell-covered floor Luther grabbed the sailor. "What's you're problem?"

The sailor knocked his hand away. "Go back home old man. This is between me an the coward."

Homer shoved his way through the crowd that was forming. "Hey, bastard, go back to your ship and sober-up," Homer said from behind. "You'll have to find somebody else to pick-on, this one's all mine." The sailor ignored him and pulled away from Homer and Luther to face Max, "You got to have old farts stick up for you, Jap lover? Nothin' but a bunch of Hooligans."

"I ain't no Jap lover, and these men," Max pointed to Luther and Homer, "are ten times the sailor you'll ever be, swab jockey. I proudly serve with them," Max rebutted.

Before Luther knew what was happening, the four sailors grabbed Max and dragged him toward the door. The small one screamed to the crowd, "Says he loves Hitler and Japan, won't fight." The patrons looked on with little enthusiasm for they recognized the state of inebriation of the sailors, and when Glen Miller began to play from the jukebox everyone turned back toward their own conversations.

Harry and Luther pushed their way through to the door. Homer had made it to the threshold and blocked their exit but one of the sailors pushed him to the floor with one sweep of his arm. Just missing the chromed metal corner of a Flash Gordon pinball machine, Homer slammed into the corner under a neon Budweiser sign.

Harry bent down and pulled up on Homer's offered hand. "You okay?"

"Go help Max, never mind me!"

Outside there was a pushing match going on and Max was outnumbered. Finally, the small sailor punched Max in the back. The large one, seeing that Max was hardly fazed, shoved Max up against the brick wall and cracked his lip with a glancing punch to the mouth. Max tried to cower down into a fetal position but two of the sailors held him up. Luther charged into the sailors. One of the sailors saw him and slammed him to the ground easily. Harry went to his Packard and pawed through the trunk for his tire iron. The sailors were taking turns on Max, fortunate for him they were mostly uncoordinated intoxicated swings.

An explosion rang out, echoing through the dark parking lot. Once again Homer shocked his shipmates. Homer put the barrel of the big revolver up to a protruding ear of the largest sailor. "Don't breath too hard, 'cause I'm an old man with shaky hands."

The sailor's eyes grew and seemed about to pop out of their sockets. Harry bent down and picked Max up, and then eased him back against the wall to allow Max to catch his breath. Finally, still a little dazed, Max stood up and offered Harry a bloody grin.

Luther put his hand on Homer and whispered in his ear, "We better get out of here before the police show up."

Homer walked backwards keeping his weapon pointed at the sailors while Harry guided Max back to the car.

Luther pushed Homer into the passenger seat and ran around to the driver's side. "Where's the keys?"

Harry reached into his pants and pulled them out, tossing them forward. Luther fumbled with them and finally got the right one and slammed his foot down on the starter button. The engine roared to life. He fought the gears into reverse with a grinding whine and then peeled out of the parking space in a cloud of dust. Luther spun the wheel on the still moving car and then slammed the transmission into first gear and pushed the gas pedal to the floorboard, the Packard squealed its tires and sped away.

Luther stole a look in the back, "How's Max?'

"I'm okay. They hit like a bunch of old ladies. No broken bones, only a busted lip and sore ribs. Mister Crown, I never thought I'd be glad to see you with that hand-cannon!"

Luther began to laugh at the image of Homer with the huge revolver at the back of the sailor's head. "Serves them right for picking on the three wise men."

Homer turned in his seat and faced Max in the back. "What did you say to those guys back there?"

"Well, after they called me a coward for not being in the Navy, I called 'em swab jockeys. I told them I was in the Corsair Fleet. They called me a pirate in a Hooligan Navy and I called them something I don't want to repeat. You guys know I didn't get too much time for discourse after that."

Harry suggested they go back to the marina to have a drink. Max wanted to scream 'to the Atlantic Beach House!'

The marina was closed but Rich Blazak, dressed in an old pair of wool trousers and a white undershirt with small yellow and gray circles under the armpits, let them in. He walked to the bar, leaned over it and grabbed a bottle of tequila and a box of cigars. The four refugees slumped down into the wooden chairs around an old poker table. Blazak tilted the candle and lit it with his Zippo, the only light in the room. They all leaned back and sighed in unison, and then they laughed at the coincidence. Everything was funny in their state.

Blazak chopped the end of a cigar off and lit it, he passed the box around.

"Hooligan Navy?" Homer asked.

Blazak surprised everyone with a reply, "The sailors think what you guys are doing is a joke. Just a bunch of hooligans making a mess of things. I suppose you threaten their position in the world, in the war. Old men on sailboats trying to find U-boats. It takes a certain kind of man to do such a thing. A real hooligan if you ask me." Blazak smiled as a circle of smoke rose up from the cigar.

"Hooligan? . . . Pass me that ta-kill-ya, mate."

Harry passed the tequila around the table, starting with Blazak.

Luther saw how Blazak inhaled the cigar in an unfamiliar way, like he was making love to it. Just looking at him, prematurely aged with a perceptible intelligence in those liquid blue eyes, Luther wanted to ask all these years what it had been like in the Great War, knowing that he could never fully appreciate the answer. Perhaps now, having the experience with the U-boat and the sight of death first-hand he could. "Rich, tell me what it was like in the war."

Blazak sat up. He looked at the others. Drawing a circle on the table with his finger he took a puff on the cigar and then watched the smoke ascend. "It was the shittiest time of my life. I never felt more alive," Blazak said still looking up at the smoke as it faded to nothingness. Finally, he lowered his eyes back to the circle he drew in the puddle of condensation. "I was up to my eye sockets in mud. Every goddamned day, mud." He looked around at each member as if to reemphasize the significance, "Mud, up to here," Blazak motioned with his hand like a salute at chin level. Again Blazak began the circle. "Disease was there along with us, just like the mud. If you didn't have typhus or dysentery you were lucky. Most came down with one or the other, or both, and then you were really fucked. And then there was the fatigue, I remember never having enough sleep, I was always hungry, dead tired." Blazak stopped the finger, "And, thankful to be alive. . . I fought with the Brits, being stupid enough to go to Canada to sign up. There was a bunch of us foolish immigrants from the City that just wanted to get out of the shithole. I think there was about twenty of us from the street that hitched rides up to Montreal. That was the first time I heard French. I tell you it wasn't the last. So, some British officer at a recruiting depot gladly signed us up. I trained for awhile with my Canadian outfit before we loaded a boat in Halifax." Blazak drained his drink and then took a drag on the cigar. He savored the flavor, but looked down to where the circle had been drawn. "I spent a year in France and two years in Belgium where it's never dry. We were dropping like flies. I think trench rot killed more than the kraut's guns. Men, these robust men from all over were sometimes nothing but a bloody mess from the waist down, soaked through. The goddamn shits—that would get you. Bloody shit, you couldn't take two steps before the urge would hit a guy and he would crouch down and squirt, because he didn't have anything solid in him anymore. They would walk around naked except for their shirts in the summer months. It was miserable life. I can't figure the sense in it all. . ." Blazak trailed off in thought. The ash from his cigar fell to the table. Blazak gave a half-ass smile. "I remember once when we were the third wave going over the top, something happened and our platoon got into the Hun's trench. We had our bayonets fixed but it was too confined to wield our rifles. It came down to us beating each other with our spades. It's a hell of a way to go, to have your brains smashed in with a shovel. Killing with a shovel is harder than you think, finally we were all so exhausted that we all lay there, us and them Huns, too tired to move. I fell asleep right in the goddamn Hun trench! I woke up when our guys came over and took the trench. We lost that trench again three days later.

"When the weather was just right we started to use gas. I was in the trench on the North side of an assault that was going badly. The jackass generals decided to gas the poor krauts. They set off a whole shit-load of the stuff, lobbing it over with artillery. I guess the gas shells had a limited range and the generals were counting on the wind for the rest. But it was blowing right into our goddamn faces. At first I tried holding my breath, but then

I had to breath goddamn it, so with unbelievable effort I crawled out of the trench just a bit too late. I basically suffered a stroke from the damn stuff." Blazak sat back, exhausted from the memories. He relit his cigar and drew on it, held the smoke for an unusually long period and then loudly exhaled as if to say, I'm done.

Luther wasn't prepared for the candid, condensed tale of the Great War. He was expecting a more poetic, introspective recollection.

Blazak took the tequila Harry held out and took a swallow. "Most of all, I remember the boredom. The waiting. Waiting for the damn whistle to go over the top."

Maybe he could empathize with Blazak. Was that what it was all about, dealing with the nothingness, the boredom, the depredation of entertainment, the silliness...patience?

Twenty-Six

They exhausted themselves somewhere shy of sunrise and headed back to Luther Rogers' summerhouse. This was not quite the Hamptons, but Luther Rogers had purchased the summer getaway when he was still struggling up the corporate ladder. He grew fond of the house and never bothered to upgrade to the more exclusive real estate on the east end of the island. The Packard ground the seashell driveway with crackles and pops as it crept toward the Atlantic Beach house, Max could only see a small portion of what must be a grand entrance from the circles ahead illuminated by the headlights. Nonetheless, the sight had an instant effect on him. He felt a sensation go through him that sobered him on one hand but intoxicated him with the other. Would she be awake?

Harry slammed his Packard to an abrupt halt in the roundabout. Massive pillars stood erect as if on guard protecting a shrine. Max had never been in a house as grand as this one. It was as if the scale of the place was out of a fairy tale and he was a shrunken visitor. Up a stairwell that made a sweeping rise around an industrial-sized foyer, Luther showed him to a guest room that was more opulent than anything that Max could have imagined. The bed that occupied center stage looked to be made for an entire family to sleep. The room had a large dresser, three chairs and enough room to hold a school dance. He made his way to the bathroom and was amazed that it held a basket with new toothbrushes, soaps, comb, razor, and shaving mug with brush. He brushed his teeth, drank a large glass of water hoping to calm the swirling motion in his head and then went to the bed. After pulling off his clothes, Max lay in his boxer shorts thinking of green eyes.

He woke not realizing he ever fell asleep. Max covered his eyes from the intense brightness that found a rent in the drapes. He sat up and then slumped back down, pulling the sheets over his head.

Someone lifted an edge to expose his face. "Are you going to sleep all day?"

Green eyes peered under the sheets at him. Max shot up, but the pain struck like the bells of Norte Dame.

"I brought you some coffee and a pastry." Her eyes smiled at him.

"Thank you, Louise."

"I'll let you get ready. I thought you and I could take a stroll down the beach, the fresh air would be good for you" Louise said over her shoulder as she slid out of the bedroom like smoke from a fire.

Max sat with disbelief. He looked down at the coffee and the warm pastry with yellow custard leaking out. He smiled at the two aspirin sitting next to a tall glass of tomato juice. He took the pills, popped them into his mouth, and then took a mouthful of what turned out to be a Bloody Mary cocktail, what a woman! The cocktail had the desired affect and soon Max was dressed in the clothes that were laid out in the bathroom for him. He couldn't remember bringing his seabag from *Lady's Revenge*, but there it sat on the floor. This was a magical place.

Banter came from downstairs. Max followed the sound and finally pushed through a door that opened to a sunroom where Harry and Homer were at it again. Luther lowered the Times, "Good morning, sunshine."

Homer and Harry stopped long enough to smile.

Louise came up behind him, "Want some eggs to go with that headache?"

Max stared but said nothing. Luther kicked out a chair for him. He sat and allowed Louise to place a plateful of two over-easy, hash browns, a sliced apple, and toast in front of him on a lace doily. But it wasn't the breakfast that he wanted to devour. He ate spying his young hostess who sat across from him, her attention devoted to her grandpapa.

"Max, now that the Coast Guard wants us all to carry the .45 automatic do you think they'll make me get rid of my Colt?" Homer asked.

Before Max could answer Harry retorted, "Homer, you need to carry a cork pop gun. You're not old enough to carry a real hand cannon like that thing you have. Probably it's the only thing below your waist hard enough. . ."

"Least I've got something hard and know how to use it. Harry, you couldn't find a . . ." Homer was cut off by Louise who rose to pour a refill for Homer more out a strategy to diffuse the conversation than any concern for his consumption of the fresh roast. "Thank you, Louise. You're spoiling me on this beautiful day."

Louise sat back down across from Max. "Oh. . .you look like you've been beat up."

Max swallowed hard and tried to smile in response.

Louise got up, "Let me take that plate for you."

"Thank you, Louise," Max said.

"Old Max here was getting the better of them sailors before Homer pulled him off 'em," Harry said with a chuckle. Homer joined in and together they sounded more like two old crows sitting on a fence.

Luther made an 'ahem' sound that indicated his plate also needed to be cleared. His granddaughter eyed him with a suspicious but adoring glare. The four men lapsed into idle chitchat about making plans for their next cruise when Louise finally cut in on the conversation. "Grandpapa, I'm going to take Max down to the beach. I think it would do his head well to get some fresh air and be rid of you three old codgers for awhile."

Foam raced up and then receded back with the pounding surf. Small crustaceans darted back and forth across the hard sand looking for food. The air was fresh with a saltiness that cleansed the senses, the breeze blew the long grass with crescendos and decrescendos that flowed as if orchestrated by some mythical conductor, Max did not recognize any of the godly beauty, save for that which walked beside him.

"Isn't it lovely here? I love this time of year, before the crowds."

Max looked down the beach and tried to count the mansions, "Not much for crowds, even if everyone were here."

Louise ignored his comment. "Why is a young man in uniform babysitting grandpapa and his cronies?"

A seagull squawked overhead. "I think they're babysitting me more than the other way around. But, I'm assigned to *Lady Revenge* for anti-submarine warfare," Max said. He surprised himself as he continued, "I watched a freighter being torpedoed a week ago. The U-boat was right in front of us." Max turned toward the crashing wave that broke on the sand a few feet away. "There were no survivors. Right off New Jersey, can you believe that. There might be a U-boat right off there, within sight. Scary isn't it?" Max asked, looking out to sea.

Louise's smile paled as she looked out to where Max pointed. "I've seen so many men go off to fight. The halls at school are empty of them, real men anyway. I feel like I'm in an all girls university." She paused and then continued, "I appreciate what you're doing, Max. Really, I do. You must feel fortunate to be here and not off in the Pacific or in Europe?"

Max didn't know how to respond so he remained quiet. Of course he wanted to be in the Pacific, where the real war was being fought. But, he was thankful to be here, right now. He felt a guilty pang tear through him. He could smell her, almost taste her.

Suddenly, an animal snort announced the arrival of a beach patrol rider, Max and Louise turned in unison. "How come I didn't get issued one of those?" the young Coast Guard petty officer asked, looking directly at Louise. He shifted the Thompson .45 caliber machine gun to the other shoulder as the horse shifted restlessly. "I'm Cullen, glad to meet you. Where you stationed?" He asked Max dressed in an identical denim work uniform.

"I'm Jackson and this Miss Rogers," Max introduced her in a way that sounded like he was introducing Miss America. Louise waved a greeting that was accompanied by her captivating smile. "Great to meet you, too. I'm on *CGR65320* at the Marina." Max didn't divulge that he was attached to the Corsair Fleet with three old men. Suddenly, Max felt the cold wet nose of a dog. "Nice dog," Max said leaning over scratching the mutt's ears as it wagged its tail. Louise stroked the horse's nose.

"Haven't seen you around, ever go to Filthy McNasty's?"

Max let go a chuckle and nodded yes. "I'm a cutterman, so don't spend too much time ashore. How'd you get this billet? Beach patrol," Max asked to be polite.

"Got lucky." There was a moment of awkwardness as Max eyed the petty officer on the horse. "Don't want to intrude, have a great walk. Good hunting," the petty officer said as he nudged the horse ahead, continuing his patrol. The dog stayed for the attention but Max finally pushed him off toward his owner on the chestnut.

Louise watched as the horse and rider sauntered off. "Pretty horse. That's the first I've seen of a beach patrol. Suppose he's looking for anything in particular?"

"It's the Coast Guard beach patrol," Max explained. "They started up recently, like everything else that's changed since Pearl Harbor. He's looking for saboteurs coming ashore from U-boats. I can't imagine the Nazi's actually doing that, probably it's for show and to make people feel safe and to keep the locals from complaining to their congressmen. I could think of worse jobs. Boring, though." Probably the only assignment more boring than his own, Max thought.

Louise listened as they walked. She liked the sound of his voice, it was deep and sounded like it came up from a dark cave, but it was gentle, not menacing. She stopped and turned and said, "Well, here we are back at the house already...I had a nice time." Louise kicked some sand as a pregnant pause wafted in the air like a time bomb, with no release or explosion she said, "I better go in and do school work. I'm sure you have Coast Guard work that needs doing."

"Thank you for the walk, Louise," Max said shaking her hand. He stood in the sand, just where the tall grass began and watched her bounce up the stairs and into the house.

Finally, he followed in her footsteps through the sand and carefully opened the heavy beachside wood-framed glass door as if to preserve the moment. "Ready, Max?"

"Ready? For what?" Max asked as he checked the bottom of his shoes for sand.

Luther pulled a worn leather attaché case from the foyer table. "We have a meeting with Commander Deemer."

"Oh shit, sorry. Let me change into my bravo uniform."

Luther adjusted his Coast Guard Reserve uniform in the mirror. Satisfied he went out to get the car warmed up. Surprisingly fast, Max slid into the passenger seat in his bell-bottom dress uniform. He had his web belt and issued .45 automatic strapped around his waist.

"Expecting action?"

"You know the new regulation. When's the meeting, I hope we're not late?"

"It's only down at the Marina," Luther replied.

Commander Deemer welcomed his task group commands to the first of many meetings for Picket Patrol, Corsair Fleet Task Group New York. "Along with the Northern, Narragansett, Delaware, Chesapeake, and Southern Task Groups, you are all that stands between Hitler's navy and the United States. I'm proud to say that we had fourteen sightings so far. I'd like to offer special recognition to

Happy Hour," that got such a reaction of laughter from the crowd that Deemer paused for it to die down. "Ted Berkley and his crew got three sightings in the last two patrols. Good job, guys." Deemer again waited for the applause to quiet before continuing. "The Southern task group actually got a confirmed sinking. A sloop on patrol off the Outer Banks was able to radio in a U-boat position to a cutter that came out and depth-charged it." This got some hoots and hollers from the Corsair commanders. "Unfortunately, it's not good enough. Up on the board I have written the casualties so far. This month we've lost twenty-eight freighters, and we're only eighteen days into it." Deemer paused, looked down at his notes, turned around to pull down a large chart of the New York area, and then looked back before continuing, "I am going to assign sectors for you to patrol. I hope to have twenty-four hour coverage of all the sectors. As you can see, each sector is roughly four hundred square miles. That's a lot of territory to cover by one patrol asset. However, with proper search patterns and by shadowing the shipping routes we can manage it. In the back of your brief sheets is the lat and long of the sectors and your patrol orders. You'll all know each other's patrol orders so there should be no confusion.

"The Civil Air Patrol has been issued our frequencies and will be flying limited patrols, so keep an eye out for them. Are there any questions?"

There was always one in the crowd, and in this crowd there were three or four, so the questions flew. Luther ignored the stupid rhetoric such as the one Pete Conroche asked, 'How come there wasn't any navy ships with torpedoes out there to sink the U-boats?' He opened the brief sheets and tried to visualize the latitude and longitude numbers on a chart.

"Jackson, how goes the grandpa boat?" Petty Officer Holmgren asked.

"Ha, ha, Holmgren. You see anything out there?" Max asked.

Holmgren looked around to see if anyone were listening, "I love this yachting. Hell of a way to spend a war, huh?"

"Yeah, hell of a way to spend a war," Max replied, thinking back to *Spencer* and the lost opportunity to fight Japs. "You're on the five-six boat with Kelly aren't you? How's he to work with."

"Good navigator. Was a merchant sailor. There's six of us on there. I gotta go, have fun out there with the ancients," Holmgren called as he headed toward to the door.

Max waved him away with a smile. Running a finger down the handwritten list he saw *CGR65320* patrol orders.

"Max, we've got to sail in six days."

Max looked sideways at the paper in Luther's lap, six days with Louise. At the Atlantic Beach house! He grunted acknowledgement. They made small talk with their Corsair Fleet counterparts as Luther and Max made their way to the door. Luther chatted with the captain of the two-one boat, and kept chatting and chatting and chatting, Max wanted to scream, 'Louise is waiting! Let's get the hell out of here!' 'Good luck' and 'happy hunting' were the catch phrases among the group. Finally, they were in the clear and back in the Lincoln heading down Lido Boulevard to the Atlantic Beach house,

Max wanted to reach over and press Luther's foot to the floor.

Luther made the turn in the driveway round-about and barely came to a stop when Max jumped out and ran up the steps hoping to see Louise waiting for him, but he was mildly disappointed. He could smell her though. He quickly changed into his denim dungarees, reattaching the gun belt to his waist, cocked his white hat like a movie star, and then checked himself in the mirror. Satisfied, he made his way down the long staircase anticipating his next sighting of Louise.

In the large den Max and the three other crewmen from *Lady's Revenge* discussed logistics for their next patrol: supplies and food, the training schedule, the orders from New York Section commander to patrol the G5 sector between Atlantic City and Long Island. They studied the charts with a grid superimposed on it representing all the sectors and their corresponding letter/number identifiers. After about an hour into it, as Homer and Luther argued about track lines, Max's thoughts wandered back to the walk on the beach.

In his daydream he grabbed a hold of her hand and spun her around like John Wayne, planting a kiss on her lips, embracing the beautiful woman in a passionate lock of two people in love.

Finally, just before he had given up all hope of seeing her, Louise entered the room and the sight of her made Max hold his breath. She announced that dinner was being served and just before exiting back through the doorway she made eye contact with Max. The facial expression was so subtle that Max had difficulty interpreting it.

After dinner, Max helped Louise clear the plates and debris from the table, and then she challenged Max to a game of chess. They played five games of which Max managed to win only one, but Louise probably let him win that one. That night Max lay awake reliving their conversation.

The next morning, Max sprung out of bed at the first sign of dawn, showered and dressed in his work uniform and .45 auto. He wished he could leave the damned weapon here, but the new regulations required him to carry the 1911A1 on his hip when in uniform, and he was supposed to always be in uniform.

"Harry, how about another refill?" Homer held up his coffee mug.

Harry turned to Max mid pour, "You and Louise walking the beach this morning?"

"Yes, Max my boy. Take advantage of Louise's hospitality. If you don't, I will," Homer said.

"Homer." Luther lowered the Times with an encouraging smirk. "Let the boy make up his own mind."

"I'm standing right here! You guys talk as if I'm not even in the room," Louise said, feigning exasperation. "I'll take him just to get away from all of you."

As Louise led the way, Max turned back to his shipmates with a grateful smile.

"Sorry about that," Max offered as they began down the beach.

"I enjoyed last night, Max."

"So did I. Even if I am a little weak at chess. It was great being able to talk with you, get to know you a little more."

Louise slipped her arm into the crook of his elbow and leaned her head on his shoulder. They walked quietly, together. The rhythmic pounding of the breakers and the music of the sea life that sailed on the morning breeze added to the tranquility.

"Sometimes it's just too much, too damned much to think about. The world has gone mad." Louise whispered just loud enough to be heard.

"Yes. . . I'll do my part. The world is crazy, the Nazis are nuts, the Japs . . . what a hell of a time to find you." Max leaned down to rest his head atop of hers, staring off into the distance down the long line of foam. "It's scary to think of the German's so close," Max said.

They continued down the beach in thought. Louise finally lifted her head up and withdrew her arm. "We should turn around, don't want grandpapa to get the wrong idea. He likes you."

Max didn't reply, he could think of nothing more than how beautiful she was. Louise stood before him and looked up with those green eyes. She reached up on her tippy-toes and gently kissed him on the lips. Max did not immediately return the kiss, but slowly he acknowledged the moment and returned the affection.

"I'm sorry, I didn't plan that. Too forward?"

Max replied by drawing her closer for another longer, more passionate kiss, a kiss that expended pent-up desires and when he finished he hugged her close and he felt the swell of her breasts pressed against his chest and the curve of her pelvis. Afraid that he might embarrass himself with evidence of uncontrollable urge he stood back, holding her at arms length. And then, he resumed his place at her side to retreat back toward Luther's summerhouse. A sense of accomplishment, or reward, and the satisfaction of achievement gave his spirit a joyous sensation that allowed him to resume their conversation. As he talked he felt truly happy for the first time in a long time. He wanted to share his thoughts with her, everything. "Don't be sorry, I'm not. Sounds a bit cliché but let's enjoy it while we can. Because we never know what the war will do to us. Everything seems so exaggerated, we don't know if the Germans will bomb

New York or invade us like the rest of Europe. How much time do we have? Sometimes I feel a sense of urgency to go fight. But right now I just want to feel you next to me as we walk the beach."

"Whoa, that's a mouthful. Very profound," Louise said just before she kissed him again.

Max put his arm around her protectively and walked back toward the mansion. Louise let him keep her close.

"Despite our great conversation last night and sharing this," swept a hand across the view of the beach, "I really don't know a lot about you, Max."

Max smiled.

"Where are you from?"

"Maine," Max said. He continued, "Let's enjoy the moment and the excitement of all of this," Max said as he swept his free arm in an arc to mimic her. "It's wonderful to have you in my arms. Let's freeze time and stay right here and let the world blow itself up without us."

Louise broke-off. "Let's not get too serious."

"Serious? There's a war going on, let's just savor the moment and let it go where it wants to go," Max said. 'Don't break it off before it even started,' he thought to himself.

Louise happily took her position back under his arm.

As they climbed the wood stairs to the Atlantic Beach home Max noticed Luther looking out of sunroom window, he quickly withdrew his arm from around her shoulders. "Oh geez, Luther's glaring at me and probably thinks the worst."

Louise just threw her grandfather a brilliant smile and waved.

Max and Louise spent almost every waking moment together while the *Lady's Revenge* crew prepared for the next voyage. They played chess, walked the beach, and stole kisses at every opportunity. Finally, the time came when Louise had to go back to school. Max stood along side the car in the roundabout as Louise sat behind the steering wheel, staring out the windshield. "I promise to write," Max whispered with a lump in his throat.

Louise nodded, a tear welling up.

Max put a hand on hers. "I will see you as soon as we get back and I can steal away," Max reassured her.

Louise moved her head up and down, the tears finally erupting. She wiped them away with her palm. "I have to go, Max."

Max fought back his own tears and stood back to allow the Buick to pull away. He listened to the crunch of seashells as the sedan drove out of the driveway, his thoughts begging her to return. He stood and gazed off in its direction not sure how to describe the sensation. The pain. The joy. He wanted to run after her.

Twenty-Seven

When the time came to get underway for another patrol, Luther let Max drive the big Lincoln back to Long Beach. With Rich Blazak's help, they loaded supplies and filled every void and spare space on board *Lady's Revenge*. Harry arrived later that day with a Coopersmith truck filled with produce and groceries—Patty had put together a menu and list of ingredients for her husband that she sent to Dominic at the company office. Harry beamed with satisfaction at the piles of stores as if he was the cat that got the mouse.

Homer was glad to see him and offered a grin that rivaled his friends. "What the hell took you so long, Harry. I'm ready to get out there, but no, we have to wait for the big shot. The businessman who brings his own truck."

"Homer go load a gun or something, better yet why don't you do some real work and help me offload this."

Soon they were underway, the four of them sat in the cockpit enjoying hot chocolate that Harry had somehow procured despite the shortage of chocolate from the rationing policy in effect.

"I think I'll make some Shepherd's pie for supper."

"Want some help Harry?" Homer asked, following his friend below.

With Homer and Harry below, Luther turned toward Max. "Max, I appreciate you teaching us about the machine gun and the depth charge launcher on the last patrol. I think Homer is especially grateful. We all sleep a little easier at night knowing you're on board. We're very lucky to have you. Without you this whole mission would be useless, pathetic."

Max shrugged.

Luther continued, "Somehow I feel as though you have humbled your efforts in the war to be with us . . ." Luther saw Max's expression of surrender and looked at the unexpected and unconnected statement float by. He had seen the scene in the bar and felt sympathetic for Max, having to endure that ridicule on their behalf. Max shifted once more to face astern. He watched the wake trail off into a slow death as Max spoke. "It was my uncle Lou who got me and my brother a dinghy-sailer. A lieutenant asked if I knew how to sail, I said sure. But I really know nothing compared to the three of you, especially Homer. Me and Doug Munro, that was my rack mate, we were going to kill all them rice eaters out in the Pacific. You know all the landing craft depositing Marines on the islands are operated by the Coast Guard?"

"No, I didn't know that."

Max faced Luther with a seriousness that Luther had not seen before and continued, "I don't mean disrespect for you guys. What you're trying to do is great. But we don't do anything out here except sail around. I guess when the war is over I'll be a first rate sailor at least. I really wanted to get those Marines onto the beach. When the Japs bombed Pearl Harbor they pissed off the wrong guy. I didn't give a hoot what they did in China, they're all the same anyway. But, they killed Americans. . . . I just really wish we really made a difference."

"I'm sorry you feel that way. But I think we are making a difference. A lot of boys are dying out here and there is no one to stop the Germans from killing them. No one except us," Luther said.

"Maybe," Max half-heartedly agreed with him.

"Louise is a nice girl."

"You're trying to change the subject, aren't you Mister Rogers."

Luther sighed affirmation, but continued, "She's impulsive. You'll never have a dull moment."

Max didn't know how to respond. He couldn't stop thinking about her. It hurt— a suffocating pain.

"Don't think I didn't notice how much time you spent together. I can think of a thousand men I wouldn't want her to be with, but you're not one of them."

"I'll take that as some sort of back-handed compliment," Max said.

A sail snapped and Luther quickly pulled on a line that lay at his feet in response. Securing the sheet in a clam cleat Luther continued, "Please be careful."

"With the sails?" Max asked, looking up at the mainsail.

"No, with Louise. She may seem strong, but she's vulnerable, a hopeless romantic."

"I promise we just enjoyed each other's company." Each other's company? What the hell is that? I want to breath the same air, hold her and never let go. . . just to occupy the same room is pleasure! Enjoy each other's company, that's an understatement if I ever heard one.

"Enough about Louise. I do appreciate you sailing with us. It must be hard for you, but we owe you so much. More than you will understand until you approach our age," Luther said.

Luther was sympathetic; he wanted Max to come with no reservations. "Sometimes our pompous and decadent American perspective on life—that almost divine sense of immortality or opinion that our death is somehow significant in the order of things—clouds our estimate of the world. Is our life anymore valuable than the hundreds of thousands of Chinese that have been killed, and are being killed by the Japanese? People all over the world are being killed by the hoards, and we Americans shrug our shoulders as if to say that is the way things have to be; besides, there's thousands more. As if people off in the remote parts of Asia, Africa, and all over are nothing but a school of mackerel. But not us Americans." Luther could have included in his argument the genocide of the Jews in Europe. Maybe Max was right, they weren't doing anything purposeful out here.

Max opened Rudyard Kipling's Captains Courageous and escaped to the foc's'l of a New England schooner. He stared at the words on the page but his imagination was off with a green-eyed woman.

"Who keeps squeezing the Colgate in the middle?" A voice from down below bellowed. Homer peeked out of the cabin hatch. "Luther, have you been squeezing the toothpaste in the middle, I hate that." Homer didn't wait for an answer. He retracted his head and could be heard delivering vulgarities.

"How can someone who is such a slob—his dirty clothes are everywhere down there—be so particular about something as trivial as toothpaste?" Max asked.

"Those are his clean clothes. I don't know where he keeps the dirty clothes, I don't want to know," Luther said with a laugh.

Homer popped out and the conversation stopped mid-stream.

Homer eyed them suspiciously, looked around and saw that nothing was about that warranted concern.

"Homer, are you ready for your watch?" Luther asked, stretching his arms over his head.

"Yeah, I can take it now if you're tired. Max, why don't you take the reins and I'll sit back and enjoy the scenery." Homer proposed.

Luther saw the difference in Homer's temperance since the brawl at Filthy McNasty's. It was unfortunate that such atrocities brought people together. He gave control of the wheel to Max who gripped it like a cautious child.

Homer took Max's place on the port side as Luther went below.

Max watched the man and then cautiously entered into the private domain of Homer Crown, "How did your family die, Mister Crown?"

Homer gave a side glancing sneer at Max, "Why?"

"I am sorry. I just thought since we're out here . . .I just wondered since you mentioned you lost them." Max let the questioning stop. They sat in silence, save for the wind and sails breathing.

"It was England." Homer said, staring forward.

Max looked at him then back at the compass and didn't press him.

Homer continued, "My wife and children, along with our grandchildren. . . all in London at the time of the outset of the war. In thirty-nine."

"Was it the bombing?" Max asked.

"No, the Germans hadn't started that yet. I took the whole family to Europe as a sort of bon voyage, farewell. See, I was diagnosed with cancer of the prostate. Later, after I returned to the U. S. it was found to be benign, however, at the time I thought I was dying. The trip was supposed to be a six-month fanfare but Hitler cut it short."

Homer sat with a thousand mile stare as his thoughts went back to those last few days with his family, with Connie.

"Connie sat at the end of the bed on a padded changing bench with her hands on her knees, I remember distinctly," Homer said more to himself than to Max. He continued, "She looked up and asked, "Any luck?"

"The Admiralty doesn't know which end is up at this point, I told her and then pulled the curtain aside to look down at Trafalgar Square in the distance, opening the brass-framed pane, blew smoke through the crack, and then asked, "Have the boys...?"

Homer came back to Max, said, "Connie finished my sentences, a habit that always amazed me, she said '—come back from their walk to Piccadilly Circus with the grand kids? No, they probably stopped along the way for something to eat. Speaking of which, we should go to the dinner room for tea.' Tea was more of a ceremony than a libation to the English, a ceremony that Connie enjoyed. But with the declaration of war three days previous, the gossip flowed hotter and in greater quantity than the Darjeeling. Connie shooed me out of the bedroom so she could properly prepare herself for Palm Court—the birthplace of London's afternoon tea. The Langham, London's first luxury hotel erected in the early years of the Victorian period, had catered to royalty and the famous, but after a depression it no longer competed with the likes of the Savoy. However, rich Americans and upper class English still held onto its nostalgic history.

"By two in the afternoon Connie, resplendent on my arm, made her entrance through the ornate brass gates into the bright centerpiece of the hotel. Filled with foreigners, mostly the damned gaudy Europeans, and an unusual amount of men in uniform, Connie and I were shown to a table in an accommodating position to be in earshot of a good number of conversations. Connie cocked her hat just ever so slightly and sat across from me with a smile.

"A waiter appeared in that trained eloquence the British wait staff have, 'Good afternoon, missus Crown, mister Crown. Pleasant day today I trust?' He leaned down in a conspiratorial manner whispered, 'We're trying to sell off the good stuff because there's a rumor the Army's going to take over the hotel for the war. May I recommend the 1907 Piper Heidsieck, magnificent champagne?'

"Connie, always enjoyed intrigue, saying, 'Taking over the hotel, how ghastly. Where shall we stay then? I'll take a bottle of the Heidsieck, some of those biscuits and the fish pâté I had yesterday. Homer, you sticking with that awful whisky?' she asked.

"I took the cigar out of my mouth, tapped off ash, 'four fingers, please, Jerome. Thank you.' It never ceased to amaze me how Connie could have four different conversations with four different tables simultaneously and not lose a beat. I sat, enjoyed my cigar and Scotch whisky while the buzz of war and the Army's appropriation of Langham filled the air like the smoke from my Romeo y Julieta." Homer paused, with longing shared with

Max, "Despite all the years, Connie still imbued that sexiness from the first time I saw her."

Homer thought quietly, admiring the heavy breasts of his wife through the lace of her blue dress a few years out of fashion. The smile and eyes and memory that seemed so real still kept Homer desiring her like a school boy.

"Homer, are you paying attention?" Connie asked, 'The Ferguson's say the Army is going to evacuate the entire hotel tomorrow. I shant think they would do that with us, would they?"

"Homer? Are you still with me?" Max asked again.

Homer looked at the young face sitting across from him, "Sorry, Max. Where was I?"

"Connie was telling you about the gossip about the Army taking over the hotel," Max replied with anticipation.

Homer continued, "I wouldn't worry, Connie,' I told her. 'The British Army couldn't give us such short notice. Really all these folks staying here, displaced onto the streets, the Ferguson's wouldn't stand for it. And besides, we're paid up until

October. I switched the subject of conversation and asked, 'what are our plans for today? When will the grandchildren be back?"

A sail snapped, and Homer cocked an eye up at the interruption but continued as he gazed up at the jib. "Connie caught on easy to my tactic of changing the subject and played along, taking a drink of her champagne. Fred and Desiree were going to take the boys over to view Buckingham Palace. Tommy is getting so big now, she said, and expressed a hope the war didn't include him. Connie went on, 'He'll be eighteen before too long, and Dave and Thad are only four or five years away. What a terrible thing to have happen when our boys are so. . . eligible.' Connie turned away as if she were about to cry, but then composed herself and turned back. 'But, Barbara wants to have me join her with Dorothy for some shopping. So that leaves you and Alex to your own devices. Think you can manage?' she asked. I remember it vividly.

"I'll take him. . .' I started to say, but as usual she continued the conversation by adding, '—to the club. I know, corrupt the boy with that boring Parliamentarian discourse.' In reply I remember leaning in with a whisper, 'How is that different than the Ferguson's political rumors?'

"Connie leaned back with a smile, 'Stop it Homer, you're so vulgar sometimes. They may hear,' she said. Connie sat back up straight, and then continued, 'I should think we could pick up some great deals with the war about to begin. Should I see if I can procure some scotch whiskey before the rationing and all that begins, just like the Great War? Do you think it will be as bad as that?' I thought for a moment, and was about to respond but the moment was lost with the arrival of a young army officer. He began measuring the room with the assistance of a sergeant. When he walked by, scribbling in his notebook, I asked him what he was doing, and he replied that tomorrow the staff was arriving to begin the process for converting the hotel into a headquarters.

"So much for shopping and tours of the city. Later that evening as we all sat around the dinner table, Connie ever the matriarch, announced the course of action,

'Your father is going to get us passage on a ship back to America. However, until that time we'll move closer to the port to await our departure." Homer shifted in his seat.

"Where we going mom,' our son Fred asked. Connie hugged Dorothy near her and replied, 'Portsmouth.' So, we packed-up that night and travelled by train to Portsmouth and arrived at the Royal Beach Hotel—our home for the next month as I spent the days trying to bribe our way onto a west bound ship. Finally, I found someone. 'Connie, I think I have our passage to America.' I told her with a great deal of relief, let me tell you. She could not contain her exuberance for the news, a huge smile plastered on her face she asked, 'who and when?' she asked, naturally. I hadn't seen the ship at this point, but an American by name of Guy Lancaster was master of it. He was trying to get out of England before the war department confiscated it. The passage cost us seventeen thousand pounds." Homer emphasized the amount.

Max whistled agreement. "What kind of ship was it, a yacht?"

Homer smiled, "I wish it had been. No, you should have seen everyone's faces when we first saw it. 'You can't be serious, Dad?' my son Alex exclaimed. Before I could reply, Connie took over, 'Desiree, Barbara, let's get our squeamish husbands on board. Tommy, Dave, Thad, and Dorothy, come with your Nana. We have to find our berths on board.' The yacht was a converted Bainbridge class destroyer from the Great War, to say destroyer is generous. The Rango Runner was about the size of a torpedo boat, surprising she could make transatlantic voyages at all. A real rust bucket with a small pilothouse up forward, but she was all boilers and no room for luxurious staterooms. With her narrow beam she had speed. So, I thought from the sight of her. We managed to find enough racks for the families, the grandkids shared the decks in Fred and Alex's suites. I think the captain displaced some of his crew to accommodate us. We sat in the mess deck under the pilothouse for our first breakfast on board when the captain, Guy Lancaster, joined us. 'So tell me, Mister Lancaster, when do we sail and arrive in New York?'

Connie asked as she stirred her morning tea in a chipped ceramic mug. The captain looked offended by the inquiry from a woman, but he replied, 'number two and three boilers are out so it'll take some time. We should be able to make the transit in about twenty-five to thirty days.' Connie never stopped stirring that damned tea, but the expressionless look was classic Connie. Alex however, inherited my lack of patience. 'Captain Lancaster, is there any way to get those boilers fixed so we minimize our exposure to German U-boats?'

"That captain didn't take too kindly to be questioned like a witness in a criminal trial, he said, 'Swim if you don't like it.' At that he got up and stormed off to the bridge. I sent Alex ashore to buy the entire family collapsible deck chairs and then made a deal with Lancaster to leave them as a gift for his crew upon our departure. Besides the mess deck there was nowhere to sit. Connie and I sat in those chairs out on deck taking in the thriving waterfront town. I remember enjoying a cigar and scotch while Connie sipped a glass of champagne, and watching Tommy chase Thad around the pilothouse. The children were adjusting to shipboard life with ease. Sitting in those damned collapsible chairs, I took and held Connie's hand. Our boys and their wives were on the messdeck playing some card game with the chief engineering officer.

"When the Admiralty permit to sail finally came, we bid farewell to England with a wave—not that there was anybody reciprocating the gesture—the old, thin hulk backed away from the pier, scrapping along a submerged camel-fender. 'Dad,' Fred gripped the handrail so that our hands touched—a subtle gesture of affection—and said, 'Thanks for getting Barbara and Dorothy out, all of us out.' I didn't reply, I didn't need to. The Rango Runner twisted around in the harbor, Lancaster was a good seaman. I watched as Portsmouth slowly slipped from view and wished her luck in the upcoming war. We headed out through the cut at Gosport, the long transit around Isle of Wight, and by time we were in the Channel it was time to eat again. Damned if it wasn't slow going, two days to exit the Channel. On the third day we were in the Celtic Sea, the Atlantic if you ask me.

"Connie rolled over in her narrow rack, 'Homer, are you up there?' she asked. I peered down over the edge of my rack down at her below me. 'I wasn't, but I guess am now,' I said. She smiled up at me. 'Want to play a little before the children awake?' So, we made love on the upper bunk in our little stateroom. It was the first time in about a week, and the last time. . . ." Homer let his head drop, staring blankly at the cockpit deck.

Sympathy gave way to curiosity. "Sorry, Homer. You don't have to continue if it's too painful," Max said.

"I felt the weight of her breasts on me as we lay there. I never want to forget that, and don't you ever forget making love to your woman." Homer paused, reached over toward Max and adjusted the mizzen sail with a tug on the mizzen sheet, and then scanned the ocean before returning his gaze to Max.

"We didn't have a shower that worked on that old tub, but we washed each other in a playful manner, dressed and reported to the mess deck for breakfast. Fred,

Alex, Barbara, and Desiree were already there in a heated discussion about the war while the grandkids tried not to act bored. We made our morning greetings, and then Connie took the woman up on deck, the grandkids stole away somewhere while the boys and I had cigars with our coffee on the mess deck. Fred thought that the United States might be able to stay out of the war, considering the outcome of the last one. Alex was for bulldozing Germany, and Hitler, under the ground. The political banter went on through the length of three seven-inch cigars. Barbara's planned family game on deck at noon disintegrated when the rain came. The entire family stood in the passageway below the pilothouse and looked out the open door at the rain that came in sideways. 'It was a nice idea Barbara, we'll try again tomorrow,' Desiree said. We all retreated to our respected staterooms. It was the last time I saw them."

Max concentrated on the rigging, fighting a strong desire to offer Homer a physical, compassionate expression.

Homer didn't seem to notice and continued his narration. "Connie and I read while laying in our racks. I heard her down in the rack below me, breathing, turning the occasional page. It is quite amazing how many sounds a person makes while laying in bed, reading. The portholes were closed on account of the rain, so when the torpedo hit, my world turned black. I was thrown about like wheat in a reaping machine. I never saw them again. Never."

A storm-petrel squawked as it passed by. Homer and Max watched the common sea bird circle them, attempting a landing on the masthead, but gave up after three tries. The bird flew away and Homer finished his tale. "When I could collect my wits, I was in the water. I was freezing. The next thing I know I was pulled up and onto a steel deck, covered in blankets, and given a fresh cup of steaming hot coffee. The absurdity of it all."

"Who pulled you out of the water, the German U-boat?" Max asked with obvious anticipation.

"No, there was no German U-boat. I soon found myself sitting at a cramped wardroom table in a British submarine. Lieutenant Commander Taylor asked me several questions, I could see on his face the anguish in the knowledge that he had just torpedoed an American ship. He told me he mis-identified it as a German patrol craft. I don't know why I didn't reach across the table and strangle him, but he didn't hide his emotions well and I felt sorry for the poor bastard. He took it hard, real hard." Homer paused and looked Max in the eye. "I can think that now, but sitting in the wardroom on the British submarine, in shock from the horror and incomprehension of just being blown up kind of put me at a loss. I didn't know at that moment my Connie, and entire family were dead."

A silence permeated the atmosphere in the cockpit like some smoking ember, part sweet, part noxious.

"Why do you hate the Germans so much if it was the British who killed your family?" Max asked.

"The Germans started this war and I mean to finish it. I don't hold any grudges against the British officer who made the mistake. He must be burdened with guilt that he will suffer his remaining days. No, it is the Germans. They didn't pull the trigger, but they created the whole damned mess and if not for them my family would still be alive."

Homer turned to face the water outboard. "You don't want to outlive your children and grandchildren."

The tale was sobering and Max felt the empathy found at the core of one's soul for the man. The urge to reach across with a friendly pat on the shoulder came to his thoughts. Max checked the compass, came a little to port, and then sat still giving Homer silence. The mainsail cast a shadow across the portside where Homer sat in deep contemplation.

"We all fight our own wars." Homer ducked under the mizzen boom and sat in the sun on the starboard side. "Harry lost his son, Luther is on some noble crusade, but what's your reason for being here?"

Max shrugged his shoulders with no apparent rebuttal. Why was he here, not sure that his reason was as noble, besides the fact that he had to be here? Caught-up in the patriotic mood of the country? Pearl Harbor? His thoughts went back to Louise. "For her," Max whispered.

"What's that?"

"Nothing. I guess because of a sense of duty," Max replied.

Twenty-Eight

The wind had abandoned *Lady's Revenge*. The sea was an inky blackness that was alive with a broad subtle swell that heaved up and down like the chest of a breathing giant. Gold spheres reflected off the surface that connected a dotted line to the horizon in the direction of the sun that seemed unable to take away the chill. Soon the sun disappeared and the sky turned an uninspiring gray.

Harry Coopersmith lay back on the cockpit bench, one foot on the port side seat, one foot on the deck. A rolled-up foul weather jacket served as his pillow. Luther stood wedged against the life rail and the cabin structure. He held a sextant, aiming at the horizon and stars. He called off the nautical celestial satellites one by one. Harry sat below at the chart table scribbling down the exact time of each and then the sextant angle as Luther barked them out. Despite his best efforts, Luther hadn't been able to get a fix the last two nights because of bad weather, but tonight was perfect for celestial navigation.

"Ready to mark Canopus?"

"Aye," Harry replied.

"Mark."

They went through the process of measuring the angles to Sirius, Vega, Fomalhaut, and Deneb. Luther liked to get four or five stars in case one or two of them did not compute correctly. He went to chart table with the times and began interpolating and reducing the angles into a useable latitude and longitude. He used two primary books: the Nautical Almanac and HO No. 229. After running through the calculations with the reference pubs he drew his lines on the chart. They intersected nicely at one point, a great fix. Now he drew a DR line out for the next three days to navigate hourly.

Luther went back topside.

"How did it come out?" Harry asked, leaning back with his head resting on his coat waiting for something to happen in the sails, some whiff of wind, anything to give them some thrust.

"Great, I feel a lot more comfortable after two days without a fix. You should come left to one-seven-four."

Harry lifted his head up to see the compass and then turned the wheel a bit to the left. "We've moved? With no wind it feels like we're going backwards. Thank god it's not blowing a gale, with this temperature the wind chill would be minus a hundred. How is everybody else?"

"Homer and Max are both out cold."

Harry laughed, "I'm out in the cold too."

Actually, Max was lying awake in his rack tossing and turning, knowing he needed to sleep. Something that Homer had said caused the deep introspection. He suddenly felt that he would never see Louise again—the thought terrified him.

He couldn't drain the thought that flooded his mind—it consumed him. What would he do when it came time to face the enemy or his own death? Would he run? Was he a coward, like the Navy sailors had said? He was stuck on a boat with three men, each with a death wish. If they spotted a U-boat, would there be no turning back? He thought of the U-boat sending a boarding crew to the sailboat. He shivered. Rich Blazak's recollection from the war, Homer's family all gone, Harry's son killed in the Pacific, Luther wanting to prove something before he dies, all his shipmates were suttee motivated—that act of a dying widow throwing herself on the burning body of her husband, or in the case of his shipmates, the memories of sons and wives, or death itself. Max felt the sensation of a child running from the hidden monsters in a darkened house. He was too young to let them drag him down into their suicidal cause. He got up, before his contaminated deliberations got the better of him, and went to the one person with whom he felt at ease, feeling an obligation to reveal his innermost thoughts.

"Max, are you writing Louise again? I'm surprised you haven't run out of ink yet," Harry said coming down the ladder into the galley.

Max offered a sheepish grin, but then went back to his missive. It was therapeutic. He felt the warmth of her presence as if they were walking the beach hand-in-hand. Furiously, he wrote, his hand not able to keep pace with his thoughts.

"Anything for breakfast? Eggs? Oatmeal?"

"Oatmeal's fine, Harry," Max said not looking up.

Harry filled a pot with water and started the burner on the stove. "I should write Patty," he said. "She must be worried sick about me."

"What's that, Harry?"

"Nothing, Max. Just thinking out loud. Should I mix some milk?"

Max made a contorted face that answered the question about the powdered milk.

Harry laughed. "Kid, you don't know how good you've got it."

After breakfast the four shipmates sat in the cockpit. "I fear a gale this evening," Homer said.

"How can you possibly know that, Homer?" Max asked.

"Don't question the wizard, Max. His father was Poseidon and his mother a mermaid. That right Homer?" Luther asked.

"Aye, but she was fish from the waist up and woman from the waist down."

That got a good laugh from the group. Finally the moment calmed.

"Chess, Harry?" Homer asked.

"Sure. I think I'm up three games."

"Like hell you are, this ain't some crooked horse race. This is a gentleman's game. Honest. You're only up two games."

"Luther, want me spell you for a few?" Max asked up through the hatchway.

"No thank you, Max. I've only got another hour on watch. Want to get the cards and I'll play some gin rummy with you."

So another day went by. The banter, the games, the meals, watch, afternoon clean-ups, the routine continued endlessly and occupied their days. Moreover, what stimulus there was to be found was found in the company of each other.

Harry was standing the 2000-2400 watch when at 2230 he called for all hands topside. The seas were pitching the Hinckley violently. She crested an eight-foot wave and the masts bent like twigs and snapped the stay rigging with loud pops. The sailboat then dove into the trough only to ride up the wall of the next wave and repeat the process. Every three or four waves the nose didn't raise, but instead buried the bow into the approaching wave. *Lady's Revenge* seemed as though she was going to dive like one of her prey into the Atlantic Ocean never to be seen again, when suddenly she sprung brutally out of the potent sea. Again the masts surged forward then savagely back as if ready to break, the sails popped like thunderclaps, and the rigging jerked taught with each surge of the mast and sail.

"I've got it, Harry!" Homer called out. "Luther, you and Harry get the mains'l reefed to the third position. Max, drop the jib and then reef the fore-s'l."

The crew followed the orders. Max slipped across the slick deck, jamming his ribs into the lifelines. It felt like he was being split in two but he quickly regained his footing and found the jib halyard and let it fly out of the cleat. The jib fell half overboard. Max pinned himself against the running wire and the lifeline as he struggled with the sail. It was filling with water like a canvas bucket. Losing his grip, he saw the halyard was caught on a stanchion. Max held to the sail and reached with his free hand across his body to the knife on his belt. He fingered the sheath with numb digits and finally got the knife and slashed up at the tangled line. On the third swipe of his blade the line parted and the sail instantly lost weight. He quickly retrieved the sail and rolled it into an unceremonious ball that he tucked under his arm as he made his way aft. He could hardly see through the saltwater that stung his eyes, the wind blowing at least fifty knots sent it across the deck with the force of a fire hose. He could see the yellow-jacketed figures of Luther and Harry as they fought with the mainsail. Max tied the cut halyard around the jib sail and then secured the line around a cleat on deck. He then jumped to the main mast just as the boat heaved upward and slammed against it.

Wrapping his arms around the mast, he clung there for a moment to collect himself but heard and saw the sail blowing and rippling loose. He undid the halyard on the mast cleat and carefully wrapped the end around the capstan. He slowly lowered it until he could see the reef points and lanyards blowing violently on the sail. Max reached out, keeping one hand on the mast and attempted to tie the reef point. The sailboat spiraled and then snapped out of the spin with such force that Max lost his grip slamming back against a stanchion that drove the steel pole up against his lower back with the power of a pile-driver. He reached for anything to keep from falling overboard. Just as he realized he was going over an iron fist grabbed him in mid-air. A wave smashed into the hull sending a thousand gallons pouring over him. Luther hoisted him back up to the deck.

The life drained out of them, Luther and Max collapsed in a heap inside the lifelines. Slowly Max stood to continue his task in reefing the foresail, Luther pulled himself off the deck with the help of a dangling lanyard and helped Max. With the knots secure at the reefing points, Max and Luther made their way back to the safety of the cockpit and together they slumped down with the utter fatigue that an endurance runner feels after a marathon. Nodding approval to his shipmates, Homer hauled in the sheets. The ride was the tiniest bit more controlled. The gale continued through the night as the crewmen huddled together in the cockpit. Homer Crown, exhibiting indefatigability, kept the sailboat pointed safely into the seas.

At some point in the early hours of the morning the seas calmed. The sun shone through a rent in the overcast sky. "Let me take it," Harry whispered, too exhausted for much more.

Homer said not a word. He removed his hands from the wheel when he felt Harry's grip overlap his own and then went below. Luther turned toward Harry with complete exhaustion painted on his face. Max watched the two men as they realized what they had been through, satisfied they made it. Max looked down through the hatch at the warmth and dryness below.

"Go below, Max," Luther told him. With slight guilt entering the decision, Max slowly obeyed the order. Once he pulled off his rain suit and the piss-stained trousers he climbed into his berth naked.

Despite the pain in his back and ribs he instantly fell into a dead sleep.

Louise.

The clanging of pots in the galley woke him, but he let his mind drift back to that dream. He wanted to go back to sleep so he could feel her, touch her, kiss her, and be with her. He lay there daydreaming about those walks on the beach, tried to draw her face in his mind. He decided to write another letter.

Max wrapped a wool blanket around himself and then walked out to the galley. "Good afternoon, sunshine," Harry greeted him.

"You didn't sleep last night?"

"I slept right next to you. Didn't budge when I shoved you over to your side of the mattress, out like a dead soldier," Harry stopped. "Like a light bulb," he said softly and turned back to the sausage he was cooking to go into the spaghetti sauce.

"You think of him often. It must be hard. . ." Max trailed off, not sure exactly how to say something that could assuage the pain Harry must feel. He tried to redirect his focus on Louise but he couldn't bring himself to do it. "What was Michael like as a boy?"

"Put some damned clothes on Max," Homer said, stepping down into the galley.

"I've got a blanket."

Harry laughed with his back turned to them.

"I don't want to sit where your bare ass has been. And God knows where that dick of yours has sailed."

Harry laughed louder.

"Homer, Max's dick better not be anywhere but in his pants. If he's got aspirations with my granddaughter he better be a goddamned virgin!" Luther bellowed from above.

"Hear that kid? You better put it away before you get any ideas with us."

Harry was doubled over with laughter, tears streaming down his cheeks.

"Harry, it wasn't that funny," Homer could hardly get it out without laughing at the situation and the exaggerated laugh from Harry. Max joined in and soon the entire boat was alive with uncontrollable laughter. Max struggled to his feet and retreated to the forward stateroom to get dressed.

Twenty-Nine

Carolina Merchant, loaded with cotton for mills in New England and raw rubber bound for Akron, Ohio made its way along the Florida Keys up the Outer Banks of North Carolina and headed for Ambrose Lightship. Machinist Mate Rickie Crane took a break from the hot, sticky engine room. This was his eleventh voyage on the *Carolina Merchant*. Rickie heard of the many stories about merchant ship sinkings by German U-boats, every merchant mariner had heard of the U-boats, but like most considered himself immune to such fate.

"Hey Mack," Dave Clarke greeted Rickie as he exited through the messdeck.

"There any coffee left?" Rickie asked, with his empty mug held out.

"We just ran out. I'll go down and get some more."

"Thanks, Dave."

Dave Clark climbed down through a series of ladders and hatches to get to the lower commissary stores.

The ship was running at darken-ship, no lights were visible out on the weather decks. Rickie flicked open the lid and spun the wheel on his Zippo, a flame came to life. He steadied his Lucky Strike on the flame and inhaled. The fresh smoke instantly satisfied his nicotine dependency.

U-251 rolled and pitched in the night swells, waiting. The shoreline was exceptionally dark in this portion of New Jersey, it would be difficult to spot any ships running dark. Fulmer had a strange sensation, he could feel a ship was nearby.

The wind was blowing a violent chill that got under the Kaptinleutnant's parka. He didn't like this. He was about to order the U-boat North when he heard the faint unmistakable rumble of his prey. The damn wind. He strained his ears, desperate for the sound to repeat itself. There! A small light flickered. Someone was lighting a cigarette only two hundred yards away.

Fulmer maneuvered the U-boat to point ahead of the oncoming ship. He quietly ordered the gun crew to battle stations. The four-man gun crew scrambled out on deck with calculated practice and prideful silence to man the 4.2-inch cannon. Below, the U-boat was setting general quarters. The engineers were preparing the diesels, making them ready to light off in an instant once the command was given, the ammo crew was opening the magazine and setting-up the relay line to the hatch aft of the deck gun. The 4.2-inch projectiles were handed up to the deck. Seven pounds of powder was handed to the loader and set on the rack where the high explosive warhead waited. Together, the two components were slammed into the chamber and then the breech closed and locked, the gun was now ready to fire. The men of *U-251* were able to fire twenty-five rounds a minute. A very efficient crew.

Fulmer reached for his spotter light and made ready to find the target for the gun crew. The standing orders stated the procedure in minute detail, the gunner would fire when Fulmer found the ship with the light. Fulmer hesitated a moment, if it were a warship he would be committing suicide. He took a second to remember everyone that would miss him and then flashed the high-powered spotlight.

Rickie Crane took a drag on his Lucky Strike, the cold night was refreshing compared to the steam room. Suddenly, a blinding light lit up his surroundings. Must be a fishing boat the morons on the bridge almost ran over, Rickie told himself as he leaned over the side in an attempt to see the trawler.

As quickly as the light appeared, another light, a flash. A report sang out. Then, a hole was blown in the hull just forward of where Rickie stood leaning against the rail. The engine room!

Rickie ran for the hatch, but the second round landed aft of him. He flew fifty feet across the deck, smashing against the ladder to the bridge. His arm hanging limply at his side with bone-jarring pain, obviously broken, Rickie struggled up the ladder. Another shell exploded underneath, lifting him up and over the rail fifteen feet to the cargo deck. He felt his arm, it was shattered and nestled against his chest. His ribs felt broken, he lifted his head up with great effort to survey the damage. The ship was ripped and torn but as he viewed the superstructure he looked down at his own body. His leg was missing! He sat trying to comprehend everything that was happening—the amputation didn't make sense. Another shell ended Rickie's pain. *Carolina Merchant* turned over, smoking, sizzling. Small explosions burst throughout the ship.

Dave Clark had three tins of coffee in his arms when the first shell hit. He thought it must be something in engineroom. He was about to reach for the door lever when a concussion knocked him back into the rack of dry goods. Cans and bags flew from the shelves. While trying to right himself, Dave heard a series of explosions. He threw aside the coffee and made for the hatch that was now oriented horizontal. The deck cantered up and he felt the strange sensation of pressure building. He heaved up on the lever arm that would open the door. He felt something tear into his left shoulder with a jolt of pain. He quickly scanned the compartment for something to use as a pry bar. Kicking a shelf until the rack fell clear, Dave pulled apart an upright stanchion and returned to the door. When he leaned down to place the end of the pole under the door lever he heard it. Pausing only momentarily, Dave frantically jammed the pole into position and then pulled up. His shoulder burned with pain, it felt like he was tearing his shoulder out of the socket. The sound of rushing water became more violent. Outside the bulkhead Dave heard the waterline move up the height of the overturned compartment.

The steel keel broke in half. The bow sank, disappearing below the surface with surprising rapidity. The stern section rolled over onto its side engulfed in large pool of oil that burned on the water's surface.

Up again he wrenched, the pole bent in his hands. He reached down and tried again on his own but it was futile. He resigned. Death was there on the other side of the bulkhead. The sound of water flowing past ceased. It became eerily quiet, but then came a sound just as frightening, the ship creaked out, screamed its death pains—the moans and agony of a dying steel soul broadcast through the bulkheads and decks. A rivet popped and small spit of water sprayed across the compartment. Dave put his head into his hands and cried. Another rivet popped. The sea filled the compartment. The cold water forced Dave to move up toward what was once the deck. It came suddenly now. He struggled into a small pocket of water, but soon the pressure became unbearable as it forced the air up. Dave had to tilt his head back so that his nostrils were just above the water level. Then it was gone. Dave held his breath and swam back to the hatch. It was black. He felt around the compartment for a door or vent or anything that would allow his escape. The pressure. Dave gasped for air.

U-251 backed away silently and then turned north.

Carolina Merchant burned throughout the night. By dawn a smoke cloud was visible from Sandy Hook to Staten Island.

Thirteen men were dead, including Rickie Crane and David Clarke.

Thirty

The welcome change in temperature marked the coming of spring, which was something Max relished about the morning watch. The early four-hour watch started with bone-numbing chills, the last hours of darkness before dawn was the coldest part of the day, but then the first rays of the sunrise reached out and touched him with an affectionate embrace. For the millionth time during the watch he thought of Louise. Max was now standing watch alone. He steered a course for Long Beach. Unfortunately, it would not be until late afternoon, if the wind kept up, until they moored.

The patrol had been uneventful, although they did get positive results with the wireless radio and managed to shoot one hundred practice rounds through the Browning thirty. Homer's tales about the America's Cup, Harry's explanations about horseracing, and Luther's description about the telephone business were fascinating after the first week or so, but by the middle of the third week the waking hours became laborious. Despite the monotony there were delightful reprieves. Homer's story about the dead duck in Chinatown had literally caused Max to pee his pants, and the way that he told the story sent the boat into fits of laughter that were more in keeping with school children than grown men.

Louise reappeared in his thoughts and on paper as the stacks of letters mounted in Max's locker. He envisioned the sight of her standing on the pier, that fine blonde hair billowing from a sea breeze and that smile that somehow seemed something out of mythology gleaming in the late sunlight. Would she be standing at the pier as before? Max continued to scan the sea for contacts while visions of Louise waiting pier-side filled his thoughts. He still could not see land, but then out of the corner of his eye he spotted something on the horizon. A white speck. He checked the trim of the sails, spied the compass and adjusted the helm a little to regain their intended course. He could see it now without the binoculars.

"On deck! I have a contact!"

The main hatch slammed open as Homer came up the ladder in sagging boxers and a dirty undershirt. He scratched himself and peed over the leeward side. "Looks like a sloop rig. Probably Kelly's boat," Homer said. He shook himself dry and went back down below. Max could hear him say something flippant to Harry about breakfast. With the binoculars Max studied the contact. It was definitely a sailboat, how did the oldest man on board spot it and properly identify it without glasses? As the minutes clicked by the sailboat came closer. Soon they were only two hundred yards off the port beam, two figures on board the gray painted sloop waved, Max returned the greeting. He studied them with the glasses and saw that it was Mr. Kelly and petty officer Holmgren.

Thirty-One

She was not waiting on the pier.

"Max, when we finish here I'm going to go visit Patty," Harry said, scrubbing the teak with a deck brush. "If you would like I could give you a ride into the city."

"Go boy, take him up on it." Homer chimed in.

Max turned toward Luther who was coming out of the hatch. "Why is everyone looking at me?"

"Luther, Harry offered Max a ride into the city. . ." Homer dangled the proposal like fish bait on a hook, waiting for approval.

"Max, I'm not Louise's father but I'm sure he would be proud to have you court his daughter. Just keep her honest." Luther said to the relief of everyone on *Lady's Revenge*. "Stay at my brownstone, I'll call Bernice make sure she has a room ready for you. Wouldn't want some bum showing up at the house with a sea bag in his hand looking for a free meal and lodging."

"Thanks, Luther, that would be very kind of you.   Are you sure that Mrs. Rogers won't mind?" Max asked.

"Don't be silly.   She'd love to have someone to dote over now that all the children are gone and the grandchildren too old to be interested in grandparents."

The drive into the city was thirty miles through most of Brooklyn, across that namesake's bridge and into Manhattan. The central borough was an impressive crisscross of manmade canyons and convoys of vehicles turning off the bridge. Harry decided to take one of the small side streets to the junction of Fifth and fight his way to Luther's brownstone. The Packard glistened with the reflection of the maple trees, that lined the street like soldiers on guard, off its polished sheet metal. Harry found an opening curbside.   "This is Luther's address, that must be his brownstone there," Harry pointed.

Max looked back to his shipmate and shook his hand. "Thank you, Harry.   I appreciate the ride, give my respects to Mrs. Coopersmith."

The Packard drove away, and was soon lost in the mix of taxicabs, sedans, buses, and trucks that clogged the street. Max stood on the sidewalk, a small canvas bag dangled from his grip. Slowly, he turned and walked up to the heavy wood door—for such an expansive city of massive steel and concrete structures, with millions of people occupying it, New York had a sobering and lonely effect on a person. Setting the bag down and comparing the numbers written on the note with those displayed on the brick, 1401, Max knocked. Suddenly a man answered as if he was waiting in anticipation just behind the door.

"I'm sorry, I was looking for the Rogers' house."

"This is the Rogers' residence. You must be the young petty officer, Maxwell Jackson?" the doorman asked.

"Yes, pleasure to meet you, sir. Are you Guy? Louise's father?"

"Heavens no," he said with a pleasant chuckle. "I'm man of the household, the butler if you will. Steven MacDonald."

"Oh, you must be Max," a woman called from within. "Luther has told me so much about you, so has Louise. Come in, come in my son. You must be exhausted after all that Coast Guard business."

"Missus Rogers?"

"Of course, call me Bernice. Steven be so kind as to take our guest's bag," she looked at it as if were some contaminated sore. "He'll be staying in Jerald's room." All the rooms were named after their former inhabitants.

Max finally stepped into the entryway, his eyes adjusted and was amazed at the deceptively large entrance. "Thank you for letting me stay here..." Max said as he took it all in. The foyer was cavernous and difficult to comprehend the dimensions, considering the deceptive width of the structure he had seen while standing at the curb looking up at the brick façade. A wide marble stairway led up to the second story and above that it continued to a third floor. The banister looked wet as if the varnish had just been applied. "Max, Steven can show you to your room. Freshen up from your road trip and then join me in the fire room, that one there," Bernice pointed to an opening that revealed a large fireplace mantle dominating a room with Victorian era furniture. "I so want to discuss your plans while in town."

"Thank you, Missus. . . Bernice," Max said, following the butler up the stairway.

"I feel like I'm in a scene from Gone with the Wind," Max whispered to Steven as they ascended.

"You'll get use to it."

"How long have you worked for them, Mister MacDonald?" Max asked.

"I've been in the employ of the Rogers for eleven years. Great people, not the usual pretentious snobs of high society. Here is your room. I hope everything is comfortable for your stay. The toilet is through that door. A linen closet is in there for your needs."

Max just stood there, admiring the dimensions.

"If there's nothing else, I'll leave you to wash up," Steven said, patting Max on the shoulder. "Enjoy," he said as he departed. To the small town boy from Maine the room could house a Boy Scout troop. Two large windows faced the street, heavy velvet burgundy curtains were pulled back to reveal white lace shades. The bed was bigger than the galley and dining area in *Lady's Revenge*. A heavy carpet the shade of the underside of an oak leaf with a deep crimson floral design lay at the foot of the bed over a deep polished wood floor. Max looked up at the small chandelier hanging from an ornate silver bracket—an obvious conversion from gas to electric. Max threw his bag on the changing bench at the foot of his bed and then went into the bathroom. The washroom was shockingly, disappointedly small compared to the opulence he had seen so far. He quickly washed his face and ran his fingers through his hair. He looked at himself in the mirror thankful he had worn his clean dress blues.

Max sat across from Luther's wife in front of the massive marble hearth. "Would you like something to drink? Coffee, tea? You sailors drink rum correct?" Bernice asked, the ever-hospitable host.

Max smiled, "I think coffee would be better suited, thank you."

Bernice smiled, "No, I suppose a man like you would drink coffee, forgive me. Tea's rather effeminate, isn't it? And, my gosh a little early for rum?" Bernice threw out the rhetorical questions.

Max was surprised to see a woman appear with a tray of coffee without being summoned. The woman set the tray down on the bear-clawed, cherry wood coffee table that appeared too delicate to support the weight. Without missing a beat, Bernice poured and began, "Luther tells me you are dating our Louise? . . . Don't be embarrassed, Luther's happy to see her finally with someone respectable. I have asked her here for tea this afternoon. She doesn't know that you're here, our little surprise." Bernice offered a mischievous grin. "So, I'll make myself scarce, I was thinking of going to Macy's or meeting some of the girls for a late lunch. Now, I don't want you to make my granddaughter . . ."

Max cut her off, "Mrs. Rogers, I have nothing but the most sincere intentions. I promise you her reputation will remain intact."

Bernice stirred here tea, "Thank you, Max. I had a good feeling about you."

"I was hoping we could explore the city together. I don't know it really. Maybe Louise could be my tour guide."

Bernice, noticeably relieved, said, "Oh, that is such a wonderful idea." She looked up at the grandfather clock that chimed eleven. "I better make my escape before she gets here. Have a grand time with our Louise. Thank you, Max."

Max sat alone. Exploring the room from his seat he noticed a leather-bound edition of James Fennimore Cooper's Red Rover resting on an end table. Absentmindedly, he paged through it with his thumb letting the pages fan by. With the book in his lap he looked back up at the clock, 11:07. He flipped the pages open again to the first chapter and then looked back up at the clock 11:08. He read, All's Well that ends Well. 11:08, time was not moving! Max examined the room, not a connoisseur of décor, it appeared to be Victorian or what he imagined Victorian should look like—

furniture made for looks not comfort. He turned back to the book and read again past the first sentence and on to the first paragraph. Newport was just up the road he thought as he read about the Rhode Island town Cooper described. Soon he was lost in the pages and forgot about the clock.

He felt cool, soft hands wrap around his eyes and stood up with a jolt.

Louise stood back giggled with that huge smile of hers, "Guess who?"

"You scared the shit out of me!" She was adorable. "Louise, it is so great to see you again."

"Max, you came into the city just for me? What a surprise! But I apparently surprised you more than you me," Louise said. She noticed the book in his hand. "Red Rover, how fitting."

Max rose and came around the davenport, taking her hands after setting the Cooper novel down. "Louise. . ." he was interrupted by a kiss.

"Yes, I missed you too," she said, smiling at him with those green eyes that drew him in.

"I was thinking you could show me around New York. And, I would like to take you to lunch."

She slid her hand into his arm in a movement that was as graceful as a dance move and led him toward the front door. "Max, I would love to take you out on a tour."

The sun seemed brighter, the air more crisp. Max felt stronger, every sense alive with excitement, more alive, more. . . he couldn't think of the correct term. . . "In love."

"What did you say?" Louise asked.

"Huh? Oh, what a great day to be alive," Max said.

Louise looked at him sideways as if he were saying something farfetched and nonsensical. But she smiled and pressed into him. She took him to Times Square, the top of the Empire State building, and then to Washington Square. "I always try to imagine Henry James's characters and where they might have lived," Louise said as they strolled through the park and under the giant arch. Max didn't know who this Henry James character was, but he was with her now not the James fellow. They made a leisurely circle around the park and then strolled down one of the border streets until they came to the intersection of Bleecker and MacDougal streets. Cafés, grocery markets, taverns, and vendors of various wares lined the street as far as he could see. Restaurants occupied each of the four corners of the intersection.

"Shall we get some chow?" he asked.

Louise giggled, "Chow? Aye, aye, matie."

They sat and ordered drinks, Max a beer and Louise iced tea. Louise said without looking up from the menu, "I missed you, Max. I think I'll have the chicken salad sandwich."

"Miss you, chicken salad sandwich?" He offered a little laugh. "I missed you too. I couldn't stop thinking about our time together. In fact. . ." Max reached down, lifted his trousers leg and withdrew the letters from inside his sock, as there were no pockets on his uniform.

"Max! I don't know what to say. Oh, I. . ." her eyes filled, and then the tears fell. Louise dabbed at her cheeks and eyes with her napkin.

"I hope those are happy and not sad," Max said.

Louise shook her head yes.

"We'll both have the chicken salad sandwich, thank you," he said to the waitress. "Louise, really it's only some blabbering from when I was bored on *Lady's Revenge*."

"Oh, Max. I've been so busy at school, I never even wrote you once."

He laid a hand on hers. She immediately placed another over his. "It's quite alright. I understand your classes and studying take up your time." They looked into each other's eyes with a perfect silence of endearment. "What say we visit the museum, I understand its one of the country's best," Max said, breaking the spell.

"Max. You don't want to see a museum, you're just trying to change the subject."

He said nothing.

"Max, I've never said this before. . .but, I'll say it now. I think I love you. I know I love you. I never stopped thinking about you while you were away. I hope it's not because of the war. It's a horrible time to fall in love, but I would have done that no matter the circumstances."

Max didn't know how to react. He wanted to jump and scream, go down Broadway like a Thanksgiving Day float yelling at the top of his lungs that he was in love with the most beautiful women in the world. The moment was broken by the waitress's return as she placed the sandwiches in front of them. "Thank you," Max managed to get out.

After they finished Max paid, and they held hands through Washington Square. Like a glowing fire in a hearth they walked hand-in-hand in the comfort of the warmth of each other's presence. Max stopped to admire the chess players, the game having become one of the staples on board the sailboat. Louise snuggled in behind him, pressing herself to his body. Max felt the passion. He felt her breasts against his back. He couldn't concentrate on the chess game two older men were playing. Do not let this day end, he prayed. Finally, they resumed their progress through the park. When they were under the arch, Max turned to Louise, she lifted her head in knowing surrender, and he leaned down and kissed her on the lips. It was gentle and not penetrating, but it grew with pent up affection and soon they were intertwined, making love with their lips and tongues.

Max felt Louise pull away as if coming up for air. Her eyes relayed the sentiment that no words could express. The moment exhausted itself and she pulled out a yellow pack of Fatima cigarettes. Easing one out, she stuck it between her lips, fired up her gold lighter and lit it. The iconic post sex ritual was not lost on Max. "Let me try one."

"I thought you didn't smoke?"

"If the woman I love enjoys it, maybe I should learn to enjoy the same vice," Max said as he took one of the Fatimas.

Max puffed on it like one of Homer's cigars, not inhaling just pretending to smoke. Eventually a few accidental whiffs of smoke made it to his lungs, he tried to suppress the cough.

"It's okay big boy. You'll learn to savor them," Louise said.

Max waved the smoke away to hide his tears and gagging reflex. Humphrey Bogart looked so damned confident and suave with a cigarette dangling from his lips, he saw his reflection in a storefront as they walked up Fifth Avenue. I need a fedora not this flat top with 'Coast Guard' written across the band.

"What are you thinking?" Louise asked.

"I look good with a cigarette. I need a fedora though."

"The hopeless romantic, okay Humphrey Bogart" she giggled as she ran her arm through his and leaned her head on his shoulder. They strode the length of Fifth Avenue from Washington Square to 1401. Soon they found themselves standing in front of Luther's brownstone. "I should get back to school. I. . ."

Max silenced her with a kiss. The swelling inside himself, the sense of wanting to combine with this woman at the core level drew him in. The embrace and passion of the prolonged kiss made the world come alive, the anxiety of the war forgotten, and joy amplified. The power seemed to subside so he pulled back and stroked a strand of her hair aside. She was more beautiful than he remembered. "I don't want you to leave."

Louise looked into his eyes. "Max, I must. I'll have you here," Louise placed a hand on her chest, "always."

Mustering some sense of propriety, Max straighten up and then looked down at his feet, this was so damned difficult. "Be off with you then. I had a wonderful day, and I still won't stop thinking of you," Max said, a truer statement never issued from his lips.

He stood at the foot of the steps and watched her walk away. She turned back twice with a smile and a wave. The blue dress swayed above her toned calves. As she reached the intersection, waiting for the light, Max saw her retrieve one of his letters from her handbag. Just as she started to unfold it the crowd pushed her out into the street. Soon she disappeared on the other side as the city traffic and Manhattan pedestrians blocked his view.

That night Max lay awake with a wide spectrum of thoughts about Louise, fantasies sincere and lustful washed over his mind like the ebb and flood of the tide. The next morning as he sat across from a bouquet of purple flowers and a stack of pancakes, Harry came in. "Good morning, Max. How went the date?"

"Good, thank you. How is your wife?"

"Patty's grand. You ready to get back to the boat?" Harry asked.

Hell no! I'm going to stay right here and see Louise every damned day, what kind of stupid question is that, am I ready to go? Max stuffed the last bit of pancake into his mouth, and pocketed it into his cheek. "Yeah, let me get my seabag, thanks for picking me up."

Thirty-Two

The meeting started at 1000, Luther sat in his usual spot as Max slid in next to him. "Good morning, Max. Thought we might miss you today. How is my granddaughter?"

"Very well, very well indeed," Max said looking ahead toward the chalkboard to avoid eye contact with Louise's grandfather.

"While you've been courting, Homer and I have achieved a great deal. The *Lady* shipshape, all squared-away for our next patrol," Luther confided.

The murmur of conversation died down as Commander Deemer strode to the front of the room. "Gentlemen, please be seated. Good morning everyone." He paused as he shuffled some papers. "I'm sure everyone here has heard about six-five-one-nine-one." Someone in the front row said, "no." Deemer continued, "It is sad. She was apparently gunned down by a U-boat about eleven miles south of the *Ambrose* lightship." Deemer waited for the reaction to die. "Be careful out there. Your job is to spot and report U-boat locations, not, and I repeat, NOT engage the enemy."

"That's bullshit Commander," Frank Henderson called out. "You gave us guns and depth charges."

Deemer raised his hands to quiet the crowd. "Those are for self-defense, not offensive action."

Luther raised his hand, but without waiting for a response asked, "Did Kelly engage the enemy offensively? Or was he just trying to defend himself?"

Deemer sighed in surrender, "The Navy pocket destroyer, *Neucomb*, en route to Halifax came across the wreckage. It appears as though the boat was hit with machine gun fire."

"Were the bodies recovered?" someone in the back asked.

"Yes, the bodies were recovered. The *Neucomb* buried them at sea. It was their only option as they had orders to proceed to a convoy departing Halifax. The families have been notified."

"You should have told us as soon as it happened! I know Betty Kelly, and Mike Flanagan is a close friend of mine." Max looked back but didn't recognize the tall redhead. The man's face turned the same shade of red as his hair as he voiced his anger and frustration with wild gesticulations.

"Men, we are at war. I just found out yesterday that's why I called this meeting. Let me relay some good news." Commander Deemer lifted up a small sheet of paper and read, "Petty Officer John C. Cullun abducted four Nazi saboteurs during his beach patrol last Saturday. The Nazis came ashore from an apparent U-boat. The FBI has them in custody. So, congratulations to Petty Officer Cullun."

Leaning in, Max whispered to Luther, "Louise and I met that Cullun guy when we walked on the beach."

Deemer continued, "This is real men. On to Corsair business, I have to give you some new patrol orders to cover the gap with Kelly's boat gone." The mention of

Kelly brought load moans and shuffling. Commander Deemer was getting close to the edge of exploding, "Give me a break! I'm just as saddened as you are, but we all have a job to do."

Max sympathized with the Commander. The reservists did not exhibit the same discipline regular Coast Guardsmen would in this situation. Holmgren was on Kelly's boat, he tried to visualize the petty officer. Could that happen to him? Not now, not now that he had Louise. He had Louise. That sounded great. Maxwell Jackson and Louise Rogers, it sounded good, but Louise Jackson sounded even better.

"Max, I'm sorry about Holmgren, I know you knew him," Luther patted Max's leg thinking him deep in introspection about his fellow Guardsman.

"Thanks, Luther," I was thinking about your granddaughter, "He was a standup guy. Hope it was quick and painless for him." Max drew a circle in the back of the chair in front of him with his finger and brushed the material to spell out "SNAFU."

"What?" Luther asked. "What's sniffaw?"

"SNAFU, Luther. It's SNAFU, Situation Normal All Fucked Up."

Luther looked sideways at him and then faced forward and nodded with comprehension. The discussion from the podium droned on until the meeting exhausted itself like a vehicle running out of gas. Max led Luther out through the crowd of Corsair sailors void of the usual small talk. The somberness hung a cloud over all of them. Following the concrete walkway, Max and Luther strode silently back to *Lady's Revenge*.

"You two look like you lost your favorite puppy," Homer said, wiping excess oil from his Colt.

Harry appeared on deck wiping his hands clean of engine oil.

"Kelly's boat got shot up by a German U-boat, all hands lost," Luther said.

"Lousy bastards." Homer pointed the handgun seaward. "I'd love to get those cowardly maggots in my sights."

The announcement cast a dark shadow of silence. No longer a dying tree trying to experience the spring of its youth, no longer the revenge of a family, no longer the therapy of a dead son, no longer the daydreams of heroically storming beaches with Marines in the Pacific—the war did what every general dreads, it planted the seed of fear. The survival instinct that was rooted in every man germinated on board *Lady's Revenge*. Each man ruminated deep within himself the news about Kelly's boat, the death of those they knew. It was out there, the monster that wanted to kill them. No amount of reasoning would change that. They were going to go out there and offer themselves to the monster. Death loomed in the Atlantic and what was it all for?

Luther finally broke the silence that hung in the air like a cold wet blanket. "We have marching orders to cover part of Kelly's patrol area, so we need to set sail this afternoon to make it".

"Aye, aye, Captain. Let's go kill some Nazis," Homer retorted with less enthusiasm than usual.

Luther bent down into the hatchway, "Harry, we ready to sail? Got enough provisions?"

"I'll run into Richardson's and get some supplies. I have some ideas for dinner I got from Patty. The diesel looks a little low on oil, we should stock up. Homer would you mind coming with me, you could get the oil while I grocery shop?"

"Yes, dear," Homer replied.

Thirty-Three

The wind was arctic as if blown off the top of the polar ice flow.

The waves rolled by, their tops being sheared off by the frigid breath of the Atlantic. It was not a gale, but rather a brisk early spring day of twenty-knot winds. Homer switched wool mitten covered hands on the wheel. His hands were now swelled clubs at the end of each sore arm, the arthritis a continuous ache that he lived with but it was becoming more difficult to endure with each new day. He could no longer imagine what it was like to not be in pain. Unfortunately, it was a part of him. Looking across the vastness the realization that he would no longer be able to carry his fair share of sailing duty struck him like the cold wind. Homer would have to find a new crewmember to replace himself.

The foresail cracked and the starboard stay wire snapped. Adjusting the sheet that ran back to the cockpit through a series of roller blocks Homer looked out past the sails, at nothing but the occasional white caps. He brought his view back to the machine gun. It was covered with an oily canvas tarp but he could make out the shape—the barrel faced outward toward the chest of a Nazi.

Soon it would be dawn. The horizon was turning blue. The seas were calming as if the sun would accept only a smooth, unruffled carpet to shine on. Homer had grown to thirst for the rehabilitating, nourishing warmth of the sun. Some of the stars low in the East forfeited their place in the sky. The blue turned to pink, to red and then white as the sun edged its way up over the edge of the earth. Finally, the morning arrived and instantly Homer's hands felt the healing warmth, the therapeutic effect of the solar radiation. Homer turned his face, feeling the sun's rays from cheek to cheek. Slowly he opened his eyes and noticed something unusual, a black cloud leaking into the sunrise far in the southern sky.

Then, unexpectedly, a thing appeared. Homer studied the strange protrusion. He thought it to be more wreckage. The far off smoke must be a torpedoed ship, and this, more debris. He aimed *Lady's Revenge* at the abnormality. The thin, upright stick had a small wake formed behind it. Was it current? Was it anchored? Never had he seen an actual U-boat, or a periscope for that matter. Questions ran through Homer's mind and suddenly he came to the realization. . . No! It was a periscope, must be a periscope!

"Everybody! Everyone TOPSIDE! WAKE-UP!"

"What are you yelling at?" Luther asked, climbing out of the cabin hatch. He turned forward to see what Homer was pointing at. He put his glasses on and saw a small thin antenna, standing out of the water about a thousand yards ahead. Luther squinted to get a better focus on the thing. He took his glasses off, attempting to clean the smudges off, but the salty film that covered the boat stem to stern also coated his glasses. Rubbing them with his shirttail he only succeeded in creating a smeared mess. The thing was moving. Luther too realized through his blurry lenses the fuzzy line was a periscope. He jumped up on the foredeck and uncovered the tarp on the machine gun and threw the oily protective cloth down the hatch. He carefully pulled back on the handle, opened the chamber latch and laid the belt of thirty-caliber ammunition on the receiving unit. The gap had been checked and rechecked a hundred times during the hours of training so he skipped that part. He closed the steel flap down and released the handle, the gun jerked as the bolt slammed home.

Harry and Max appeared out of the cabin door. Harry looked out at the beast that was under the surface only detectable by the protruding appendage, backed up and eased himself onto the cockpit bench. Max just eyed the creature, frozen in the spot, mouth agape.

Homer was at the helm. He studied the distance and the eye turning ever so slowly. He forced down his curiosity of the monster, knowing he had to position the boat. Then, with convincing sight and quick calculation of the time/distance movement of the Nazi beast, he called out, "Come-about, haul in the sheets and make America's Cup speed!"

The periscope turned as *Lady's Revenge* slammed into the cross sea. Homer swung the wheel, the spokes disappeared in a blur. The arthritic pain was gone. The Hinckley heeled to port and sliced through the water. Spindrift sprayed up over the gunwale as the shrouds buzzed. Luther braced himself against the sudden heal. Harry hauled in the jib sheet. Max did not move. Homer continued to drive the boat counter clockwise around the rotating periscope.

The periscope stopped moving, as if it saw something. It was the break they needed to close the distance.

"We're crossing its bow! It's going to see us!" Max screamed.

"Ready to come about!" Homer called out. "Hard-a-lee!"

Lady's Revenge responded sharply. The sails crossed the midline as the booms sped across the decks toward the opposite side. The Hinckley, with no loss of momentum, was full speed on a starboard tack. A wave pounded over the bow. The jib absorbed the saltwater. For the first time, Max witnessed the remarkable seamanship that proved Homer's god-like sailing abilities and why he was the best damn sailor in the world. Luther and Harry hauled in the port jib sheet to trim up the foresail.

Max never took his sight off the onrushing periscope. Louise. "We're in its torpedo path. We have to get out of its way, we need space for an attack!"

Homer felt the adrenaline flowing through his veins. He gripped the mainsheet in his teeth, hauled in the mizzen sheet, dropped it and did the same with the mainsheet. *Lady's Revenge* lurched forward from the more powerful trim.

The periscope paused directly astern. Then, slowly it continued its rotation. The periscope was coming around too fast. It was certain to see the 65-foot Hinckley.

"Come on *Lady*," Luther encouraged the sailboat like a lover.

Homer braced his feet against the bench seat. He turned into the wind ever so slightly. "Get your lard-asses to port!"

Max and Harry jumped for the portside lifelines.

Homer couldn't reach the winches. He pulled back on the sheets. Max was amazed at the sight, awed as the eldest member of the crew defied the power of the sails.

Homer turned toward the periscope and trimmed the sails even more. The periscope was speeding toward the *Lady* at eight knots. *Lady's Revenge* was cutting a path in the ocean at fifteen knots. The two vessels were going to collide. Homer willed the boat to go faster.

Luther glanced back at Homer and then returned to the periscope. "We're going to hit. Brace yourselves!"

The periscope had only twenty degrees more of rotation and it would see the gray hull of the Hinckley in its lens.

Homer pressed the threshold of his trim even further. He turned into the periscope.

Max closed his eyes. The periscope was hid by the bow. Harry gripped the lifeline with white knuckles.

Homer leaned back and pulled one more inch of sheet through the clam as the periscope raced along the hull. With brilliant speed and maneuver, the periscope passed just inches from the transom. They made it. *Lady's Revenge* had escaped undetected.

Max lunged for the racks. He quickly dialed in fifty feet and pulled the launcher arm. The air popped and sent the depth charge skyward, it splashed down over the U-boat. But it did not go off. They waited, holding their breath, nothing.

"Why the hell didn't it explode?" Max yelled at the apparatus.

Harry came up next to him and whispered, "Did you arm it?"

"Of course it was armed, it must've been a failed charge. Probably surplus shit they gave us."

"It's coming up!" Luther yelled.

Luther watched as the periscope rose higher, it was followed by a large cylinder platform, and then the tip of its bow broke the surface forward. Soon he was staring at the net teeth and deck gun and conning tower followed by the entirety of a German U-boat.

Homer didn't know how he was going to sink the Nazi bastards, but he kept the

Hinckley on a close reach into the mouth of the waiting, unsuspecting monster.

Luther pointed the Browning at the U-boat. He was uncertain where to aim. He had hoped that someone else would be at the trigger. He could sail after U-boats, but could he shoot one? His hands were cold and sweaty. The grip on the machine gun was slippery. His finger rested gently on the trigger, but the trigger wouldn't move.

The U-boat was moving slowly into the advancing sea, oblivious to the silently approaching sailboat. No one spoke. All eyes were transfixed on the surfaced beast ahead. Suddenly, they heard someone opening a hatch, that characteristic unscrewing sound of the braces being retracted. Soon the deck was covered with dark figures running across the U-boat.

"Let's get the hell out of here!" Max cried.

Homer held his course. Max saw the boat wasn't changing its direction.

Homer, Max, and Harry turned in surprise as they heard the machine gun come alive on the foc's'l and saw Luther Rogers crouched low behind the sights.

Smoke appeared on the deck of the U-boat followed quickly by thud and thwap sounds of lead projectiles impacting the Hinckley. Wood debris turned into missiles. They were being shot at!

Luther kept his finger clenched around the trigger. The large water-cooled barrel was lost in smoke. The gun resonated as round after round poured out. Luther couldn't see his target through the smoke. He was horrified. Terrified in a way he had never before experienced; as if not only his own life were at stack, but that of his family, his country, and the entire world depended on him at this moment. The fear paralyzed him, but his finger would not budge from the depressed trigger.

The last empty casing hit the deck and finally the smoke cleared. Luther stared out. The U-boat was gone.

"You did it! You scared the U-boat away! Did you see that? Bullets flying everywhere, they were scared shitless. I can't believe that. Yeah! Who needs to go to the Pacific!" Max cheered as he ran forward toward Luther.

"Max, will he come back?" Harry asked.

"Ah, well . . ."

Homer added, "He will won't he?"

Max was ecstatic that Luther had forced the U-boat to submerge with just a .30 caliber machine gun. But, now, he admitted the U-boat was probably submerging to ascertain an attacking position. He did not want to think about facing the U-boat on their terms. They had to act fast.

Homer demanded, "It will won't it?"

"Yes, I guess it will. And, this time it won't scare so easily."

"Can we attack?" Harry asked.

Luther listened quietly.

"With depth charges?" Homer added

"I think."

"We can't waste time sitting here thinking about it! Let's do it," Luther said, standing up on the cabin roof.

"Mister Rogers, do you have a position on the U-boat?" Max asked the Captain of the boat. The last Mk6 depth charge was a dud so Max was skeptical.

"I would say right about there." Homer pointed at the spot he guessed where the U-boat hid.

Max's mind focused, all his efforts and thought centered on one thing. "Homer, steer a course that will put us about two hundred yards away on a parallel course. Harry, help me with the depth charges."

Harry looked at Homer and asked sympathetically, "Homer, do you want me to take the helm so you can do the depth charges?"

Homer was starving to shoot a Nazi or shove a depth charge down his throat, but, he knew the importance of his position at the helm: he was the best sailor of the four, and Harry Coopersmith was twenty years his junior. "I better stay here at the helm. If I give it to you, you'll have us aground on the next tack. Thanks, Harry."

Max glanced up at Luther standing above the crew like a giant redwood. "Mister Rogers, you'd better reload and man your gun."

The wind seemed to sense the shift in determination on board, it gusted, giving *Lady's Revenge* attacking speed. The hull slapped into the waves with a roar. Luther wished for silence. Surely the U-boat could hear the Hinckley thundering through the crest of every wave. The sails were taught and creaked from the strain.

"Dial in the depth fifty feet, she probably won't be deep. Must be careful, though, not to sink ourselves with the explosion."

Harry turned the ratchet on the face of the depth charges.

The water churned as the U-boat surfaced again. This was unsuspected. The deck was washed clean with saltwater as the steel leviathan reared. Luther struggled with a fresh belt of ammunition as he saw men appearing out of the hatches on deck. A man on the conning tower fired a machine gun that sprayed water around *Lady's Revenge*. Wood splintered across the deck.

Crack! Whoosh! Max and Harry watched together as the depth charge flew from its cradle toward the surfaced U-boat. The drum cleared the deck of the enemy and splashed into the water on the far side. It was an eternity of nothing. The German machine gunner stopped firing, Luther ceased his struggle with the ammunition. All that were on this deadly stage waited motionless with anticipation. Then it came. A dull thud shook the entire sea, and then a geyser of white water shrouded the U-boat. *Lady's Revenge* rocked violently from the shock wave. Down below dishes crashed, books and charts, cards, a cribbage board, lanterns, the radio, and any unsecured articles found their way to the deck. The power of the explosion had been unexpected. Even Max was surprised at the shock wave that hit the sailboat. The Hinckley was picked up and tossed over a fleeing wave. The keel cut into the water, the hull slammed down, and then water sprayed outward in all directions.

To everyone's amazement, the Hinckley sailed onward.

Luther looked up over the lifeline he was clinging to—the U-boat was still there. It had also survived. He felt a pain in his chest. A wave of defeat washed over him, the U-boat would use its deck gun to destroy *Lady's Revenge*.

"It's going down!" Max cried out.

The U-boat was slowly, but definitely sinking. The men on deck were no longer concerned with destroying the unworthy little sailboat, they were scurrying about trying to save their doomed submarine.

Harry, Luther, and Max looked on, uncertain what they should do. It was like gazing into a microscope seeing the battle for life of an amoeba as iodine rushed across the slide. Harry answered the solemn mood.

"We have to kill them."

Homer, sitting in the cockpit his legs spread awkwardly out across the deck, agreed.

"Homer?" Luther asked, looking at his friend's pathetic position and expression.

"I'm afraid I've been hit pal. Run right through." He opened his hands that were holding his abdomen, revealing a stain of blood. "I can't move my legs." Homer did not feel the glory of battle that had driven his fortitude earlier, but he simply resolved to complete the task.

Luther saw a crimson red puddle form where Homer sat. He looked back at the U-boat with vengeance. The deck lay just beneath the surface of the water. He turned to face his crew. "Let's set up another attack. Homer, I'll help with the helm."

No one spoke. The devastation that struck *Lady's Revenge*, that struck Homer Crown in the spine, offered no opportunity for conversation. No one could think of anything possibly consoling. What do you say to a man, a friend that just had his spine shot to pieces and was bleeding to death?

The boat responded well. Luther brought the Hinckley around on a port tack. Harry and Max were poised ready for the launch that would end their foe. Homer looked at the U-boat, smiling through his tears.

The conning tower of their enemy protruded out of the ocean like a tombstone marking a grave. The sailboat rushed in towards the beast. The jib was not properly trimmed but no hands could be spared to correct the deficiency. The hands of the sea were at the starboard quarter pushing the *Lady* forward. Luther felt a pressure build again in his chest. The moment was near as his hands trembled at the wheel. The monster that had ravaged the East Coast was a thousand yards away and closing. Luther had seen the might of this creature now he could smell the fire on its breath. He was not certain whether the giant redwood was growing or falling. The boy with one leg in the train station was far away and long forgotten. He wanted to be home, in his office, anywhere in the world, but not here. His brow was letting sweat fall down into his eyes.

"You're getting too close. Hold off a little so we can drop it right down on his lap," Max said.

Luther nervously adjusted the helm.

Max hit the release level that caused a loud metallic hammer sound. The launcher failed. The explosion and subsequent shock wave had ruptured the air seal that held the pressurized air needed to hurl the heavy depth charges. Max repeated pulling the launching arm as if it would miraculously repair itself. Harry looked on helplessly.

"What? What is it, Max?" Homer asked.

"The launcher won't fire the damn drums, something must've happened to the air. The explosion must have damaged something."

Luther turned off the target, almost relieved, but disappointed.

Homer watched in disgust and impotency.

The U-boat coughed up a dark ball of fumes. The conning tower formed a wake behind it. It was underway!

The Coast Guard crew watched in silence as the beast sailed away. Sitting on the bench in the cockpit, Luther put his elbows on his knees and stared at the gray deck. The crew looked at their Captain.

With sudden resolution, Luther stood and said, "Harry, get the life raft out, ready, and over the side. Homer, can you hold the helm?" Homer nodded. Luther continued, "Max, help me roll one of those depth charges to the bow."

Max obediently dropped a depth charge off the rack and rolled it, somewhat clumsily to the bow. He latched it to the lifeline with a piece of jib halyard. Harry surfaced out of the lazarette with the compressed life raft and pulled the pin, releasing the CO_2 cylinder. He gently lowered the rubber raft into the water, holding on the lanyard that circled the circumference. Homer watched, and like the others he said nothing. No one dared ask Luther just what-in-the-hell he was up to.

All of the orders fulfilled, the crew waited for further instruction from their Captain.

Luther walked to the bow, tested the weight of the depth charge and returned to the cockpit and the anxious crew. "Harry," Luther shook his hand oddly, "get in the raft. Max, get in the raft with Harry."

Harry bent down and kissed Homer on the forehead and then whispered, "Bye my friend." Max and Harry entered the life raft not questioning Luther's orders. Homer looked on as his blood was starting to collect in the bottom of the cockpit. Luther looked back at the U-boat then at his friend, "Are you up to this? Can you hold the helm?"

"Yes." Homer said.

Harry and Max remained silent. They gazed up at Luther. He released the raft from the *Lady's* hold, setting it adrift. "We have to finish it," he called to them.

Harry spied the New Jersey coast. Harry and Max sat in the bottom of the rubber raft with silent acceptance of Luther's decision. The solemn moment lasted an eternity as the two drifted apart. Luther gave one long last look then turned his attention to the more pressing issue at hand.

No words were passed vocally with Homer, but an entire epic was conveyed when their eyes met. Luther glanced down at the crimson puddle that was growing and then back at his friend. He hoped that Homer would have the strength to hold his course. Luther pushed down his emotions and walked forward along the lifeline.

The U-boat switched to battery power and was beginning to dive to make its slow escape.

Luther could just see the antennas and periscope sticking out. Homer managed to pull in the sheets with his arms that had just enough strength left in them. *Lady's Revenge* pushed ocean aside as it raced through the waves toward the underwater monster. Luther untied the depth charge. He sat, ungracefully, with his legs spread and hanging over the gunwale. He hugged the depth charge in his lap. *Lady* charged.

Luther Rogers felt the redwood rise to astronomical heights. He knew that when it fell, it would be for the last time. It was Elysian enrapture, a somewhat welcome loveliness—the threshold of death.

Finally, they caught up to the U-boat and Luther calculated when they should be right over top of it. Looking down into the sea, his shadow and the depth charge mixed with the silhouette of the U-boat underneath. Luther pushed with all his might and let the drum fall. It splashed and disappeared below. He waited for the explosion, wondering if it would be painful.

Max and Harry looked on and then saw Luther release the depth charge into the sea with a splash. They waited for the eruption that would signal the end of their friends. Harry grabbed Max's hand and squeezed firmly, they held together for the inevitable. But it did not come.

Luther hurried to the stern. He pulled the release lever, the remaining depth charges splashed over board. Again there was no explosion. Had he forgot to arm the drums? The Hinckley raced onward and past the submerged U-boat. It took all his effort but somehow Homer concentrated on the sailing. Luther looked back and saw that Homer was drained, pale, and near the end. He walked back toward his friend and eased himself down into the cockpit. Under Homer and along the port side, the upholstered benches of the cockpit were covered with blood now dark and hardened. Homer's wound was matted and ugly. The blood was clotted but he was still hemorrhaging, small streams seeped through the canyons formed of dried blood in the folds of his shirt. Luther pulled his friend's hands off the wheel and set them in his lap. Homer was still.

Luther turned *Lady's Revenge* to port toward Max and Harry adrift in the raft.

He quickly reached them and let go all the sheets and threw them a line. Once they were back aboard, Max and Harry carefully and without a word deposited the body of Homer Crown under the spare jib sail. Luther pulled up blood stained and caked cushions and threw them overboard and then drew a bucket of water in and washed down the deck. The blood stained the gray deck brown. The cleansing of death cast a horrible sense of accomplishment over them. They all sat after the chore was complete.

The shadow of the sail was not sufficient enough to hide Homer Crown's body.

"Should we follow the U-boat?" Max asked.

Luther could not speak. He had lost more than a friend.

Harry answered, "I do not believe we can prosecute without depth charges. We should get to shore quickly to. . . Homer needs to be attended to, buried."

"No."

"Excuse me, Luther?"

Luther gazed at a lock of hair waving from underneath the sailcloth. "Homer Crown shall be buried at sea. His family is here. He shall return to that which was his life."

"Harry," Max began, as if Luther was no longer in their company, "can we bury him out here without telling someone? Is that right or even legal?"

Harry thought for a few seconds. "Luther's right. What is proper would be to put him to rest out here. It doesn't matter what people ashore will think, relaxing in their comfortable houses gloating in the prosperity brought by the war, what matters is Homer and what we're doing out here. We should do the right thing. I agree with Luther, everything that this man was is here at sea. It is only fitting he be buried out here. But how do we bury him?" The thought of once again touching the dead body did not agree with Harry's disposition. But he was beginning to be exposed to a lot of uncomfortable situations.

"Max, can you rig something to bury him in?"

Max nodded and went below to find twine and needle, and the necessary items to bury a body at sea.

"Luther, let me take the helm," Harry said.

Max went below and unbolted the air pump that had been damaged in the attack. A bullet hole had cracked the casing rendering it useless as a pump, but not for a funeral. "Luther! We're taking on water!" Max yelled out as he noticed the deck was at water level, it squished when he stepped on the boards hiding the bilge. He lifted the deck plate and saw nothing but water.

Luther came down to investigate the flooding. He knew it wasn't that serious if it remained at that level. He ensured the bilge pump was clear by reaching down into the black water to feel the pick-up strainer. It was clogged. He pulled out the obstruction, a piece of cloth he could not identify. Starting the bilge he could soon hear the reassuring sound of the stream of water exiting outboard. Luther returned to his task above.

Max spread the extra jib sail out beside Homer's body and gently rolled the man inside. Pulling the last stitch closed, Max set the weight of the body down onto the deck. He then tied a timber hitch around the middle of the sailcloth, and, sitting on the transom, attached the other end of the line to the wasted k-gun pump.

Luther and Max gently moved Homer to the stern so he could be easily pushed overboard.

"Damn good sailor, he was." Harry said.

"And a grumpy ol' fart. He was an honest, decent man, I guess you can't say much more about a man than that," Luther said, but knew it was not a fitting epitaph.

"May I?" Max asked, proffering his Coast Guardsman Manual. Luther was delighted to see the blue book. Max read, not from the printed pages, but from an inscription in the back, written by John Masefield, a shipmate.

I must down to the seas again, to the lonely sea and the sky,

And all I ask is a tall ship and a star to steer her by,

And the wheel's kick and the wind's song and the white sail's shaking,

And a gray mist in the sea's face and a gray dawn breaking.

I must down to the seas again, for the call of the running tide

Is a wild call and a clear call that may not be denied

I must down to the seas again, to the vagrant gypsy life,

To the gull's way and the whale's way where the wind's like a whetted knife;

And all I ask is a merry yarn from a laughing fellow rover,
And quiet sleep and sweet dream when the long trick's over.

Max closed the book. Luther rolled Homer over. The body splashed and dragged behind, Max nudged the air pump off after him with a kick. It took Homer down quickly. He was gone.

Epilogue

Admiral King finally admitted that there was a problem on the East Coast when he released the Atlantic Fleet to Admiral Andrews who began an extensive anti-submarine war against the Germans. From December 7, 1941 until June 1942, 259 ships met their death within sight of the East Coast of the United States. That number might have been higher if not for the courageous efforts of the men in the Corsair Fleet.

Lady's Revenge made it back to Long Beach with her remaining crew. The Coast Guard decided the Hinckley was not worth the cost to repair the damage caused by the underwater explosion of the depth charge and the U-boat's machine gun. Luther put her up in a cradle until he sold her eight years later to a charter service that rebuilt the ketch and moved it to the Caribbean. It served as a barefoot charter boat until 1967 when a couple from Chicago ran it aground in St. Nevis where it ripped apart on a reef.

Maxwell Jackson finished the war as a LST coxswain aboard the *USS Niagara Falls*. He was wounded taking U. S. Marines across the wide coral reefs at Asan beach in Guam. He married Louise in 1950 they have four children. Max continued to race sailboats and received a lifetime membership to the New York Yacht Club as directed in the will of Homer Crown. Max died in 1961 when he was struck by an intoxicated seventeen year-old while driving his Chevy through a busy intersection in Baybridge, N.J. Harry Coopersmith was a pallbearer.

Harry Coopersmith sold his racetracks and helped reorganize the struggling National Football Conference. He negotiated contracts for the newly formed NFL that allowed its survival in the transition to television. Harry Coopersmith died of prostrate cancer in Marathon, Florida in 1971.

Luther Rogers moved out of the city to Deer Isle, Maine. He began making wooden sailboats and started Deer

Boatworks. He set sail in 1963, at the age of ninety-two to test a new hull design named *SNAFU*, he was never seen again.

Kapitanleutnant Fulmer did get awarded the Iron Cross for his valorous action in the Western Atlantic 1942. *U-251* made it back to Germany. She sank with all hands off the cost of Sicily in 1943.

The author used some artistic license in John C. Cullun's capture of four Nazi saboteurs that actually occurred on a Long Island beach, July 25, 1942. The *USCGC Spencer* was not actually ported in Boston, but instead its real homeport was New York before the war.